I found Monty on our front steps. He looked scared when he saw me. My free hand was balled in a fist, and with the other I slung the green bag of returnables right at him.

"There's our money," I said. I jabbed my finger in his face. "We do not run. Do you understand me? You're never going to run again. You won't be afraid of anything or anybody. . . . "

"I'm not afraid," he said weakly.

"I'm going to teach you. You can't run anymore."

Monty sighed. He tried to sound like he was bored with me, but he was terrified. "What's it, time for a lesson now, George? We going out back for a lesson?"

I brushed by him on my way into the house, without looking at his face. "Monty, I can't take you out back when I'm angry. If we go now, I'll kill you. You missed your damn lesson today. I can't show you anything about toughness the way that guy could have. Want to see somebody tough? Want to see a guy who can take care of himself? Go back to Frank's. Now stay out of my face."

Also by Chris Lynch

Iceman

Gypsy Davey

Shadow Boxer

Chris Lynch

*To the Travelling Gantosburys,
Good luck way down here.
Be brave.*

Chris L

HarperTrophy
A Division of HarperCollinsPublishers

Shadow Boxer
Copyright © 1993 by Chris Lynch
All rights reserved. No part of this book may be used or reproduced in
any manner whatsoever without written permission except in the case
of brief quotations embodied in critical articles and reviews. Printed in
the United States of America. For information address HarperCollins
Children's Books, a division of HarperCollins Publishers,
10 East 53rd Street, New York, NY 10022.

Library of Congress Cataloging-in-Publication Data
Lynch, Chris
    Shadow boxer / Chris Lynch.
        p.   cm.
    Summary: After their father dies of boxing injuries, George is determined
to prevent his younger brother, who sees boxing as his legacy, from pursuing
a career in the sport.
    ISBN 0-06-023027-4. — ISBN 0-06-023028-2 (lib. bdg.)
    ISBN 0-06-447112-8 (pbk.)
    [1. Boxing—Fiction.   2. Brothers—Fiction.   3. Fathers and sons—
Fiction.]   I. Title
PZ7.L979739Sh   1993   94-47490
[Fic]—dc20   CIP
                                                                        AC

First Harper Trophy edition, 1995.

To my brother Marty,
who contributed much to the making
of this book
but won't be getting paid for it

Contents

Prologue: Rocks

I was nine years old, younger than Monty is now, the first time I hit my father and made him bleed. He was proud.

"Atta baby, atta baby!" he screamed without looking at me. He was staring into the little puddle of blood that was gathering in the palm of his glove. It wasn't that cutting his lip was such a hard thing to do—he opened old cuts every morning just brushing his teeth—it was that *I* finally landed the big punch.

"Sorry, Dad," I said, too scared to notice how happy I'd made him.

"Sorry, shit, Georgie. Tha' was great. Don' never apologize for doin' it right. This is the point. If you ain't trowin' a punch wi' bad intentions, you shouldn't be trowin' it."

That was the day, almost five years ago, that I picked up on bad intentions. Until then I was happy to bounce punches off his gloves, run in circles around him while he threw pillow-punch jabs at me. I was happy to get up with him at five in the morning and tail after him on my bike while he did his roadwork. I was happy, dammit, to carry his water bottle, hand him the spit bucket, lace up his tall shoes that only the fighters wore. He was my dad. I'd have been happy just to *be* his spit bucket.

But it wasn't good enough for him. He had things he had to show me.

"Right here," he said, punching himself in the chin as he closed in on me. I threw the jab, but his gloves were already there to catch it. He always fought peekaboo style, hands by his cheekbones, bobbing, bobbing. I only came up to his bottom rib, but when he was in his crouch, I could reach him.

"Faster, Georgie," he yelled, exposing his face again. "Ain't nobody gonna wait around for you." I lunged, hitting the gloves again. "George!" he yelled. He never used to yell at me. I dropped my hands. "What's wrong witcha, boy?" He got madder, rushed me, took advantage of my lowered guard. With open-handed slaps, he started cuffing me all around the ring. One-two, left-right, one-two, he chased me around the ring as I back-pedaled. "Georgie," he kept saying, "Georgie." I didn't understand what was so wrong. My cheeks were starting to sting like they were windburned. "You don't have time for pitty-pat anymore, son," he said. "Bring them hands up."

And as he said it, he brought his own hands down. When I saw it, I didn't have to think. I threw my whole body behind an overhand right, leaving my feet, aimed right at the lip scar I'd seen spill so much blood before. When my hand stopped cold on my dad's mouth, my bones ached all the way up to the shoulder. But it wasn't a bad pain. I wanted that scar and I got it. Bad intentions.

When he stopped cheering, he grabbed my face between the two soft, overstuffed gloves he wore just for me. I could feel the blood in his palm, warm on my cheek. He couldn't stop grinning, a real goofy, funny grin without either his mouthpiece or his front teeth in. "Could ya do it again, do ya tink?" he said, all excited.

We scuffled for a couple more rounds. I hit him a lot after that. A couple of times I think he let me sneak one through, but just a couple. He didn't believe in that. Mostly, I just figured it out, all the things he'd been teaching me for as long as I could remember: Take the body, the head will follow; focus, pay attention, and the other guy will show you where he can be hit; don't drop your hands for any reason; don't stop moving; and when you throw that hand, throw it for real.

My father actually giggled when I hit him hardest. It was the happiest day in his whole life, at least as long as I knew him. Not that he wasn't a happy guy; he just didn't laugh much when I knew him.

We stopped when Dad's brother Archie came in with a couple of kids. Archie was the one who actually ran the gym, but whenever he, or anybody else, came in to go to work, Dad always took me out.

"C'mon, young man," Dad said, spreading the ropes wide for me to step through. "We got roadwork to do."

"Great," I said. "I'll get my bike."

He hopped out of the ring behind me, slipped off a glove, slipped in his teeth. "Uh-uh," he said, chomping the teeth into place. "Bike's for kids. You're runnin' wit' the old man." He slapped me on the back and walked toward the exit. Walking was tough for him. Both feet pointed left and he looked to be constantly sort of falling off to his right. The problem was just with walking, though. He could run forever.

It was kind of stretching things to call it road-

4

work, anyway. We just jogged the four or five blocks home from the gym, nothing like the six-mile sunrise runs. Still, I was pretty juiced about it.

"Roadwork sucks, Georgie, but you gotta do it," he said as we trotted side by side, shoulder to hip. "There ain't no shortcuts, so don't go lookin' for none."

"Okay, Dad, I won't," I huffed, like I would have written it down if I had a pencil. He had always given me these pointers—rocks, he called them—but they seemed to be coming like an avalanche lately.

We didn't run the straight route home exactly, instead slanting down Amory so we could hit the boulevard that ran along the beach. It wasn't a great beach, in the town we lived in back then. You wouldn't go there to swim or anything. But when it was early and gray out, with nobody there but the sea gulls eating garbage, there couldn't have been a finer stretch for a guy and his old man to run.

Dad blocked his right nostril with his fist, then blew out the left onto the sidewalk. "Good day in the ring today, son," he said. I was struggling to keep up but I heard him just fine. He spun and started running backward, looking right at me as we went. "You make me feel that maybe I done good, bringin' you along."

"You done great," I said. "So why is it that we always have to leave when the gym opens up? Huh, Dad? Why can't we stay and do more, hang out, so I can learn everything there is?"

He stopped running, stuck out his hand like a traffic cop to stop me. "George, ain't no way. *Ain't no way* you gonna be no gym rat. Understand? I swear I'll swallow you whole first."

He didn't play, my dad. So when he stood there with his big hand pressed flat against my chest, I knew then and forever that I wasn't going to be any fighter. When I cut his lip, Dad promoted me to Man. But when he scooped me up by the armpits and stood me on the sea wall, he brought me back to being his boy, too.

"Here's a rock for you to keep, Georgie," he said. "The fight business gave me one thing, an' I give it on to you—it made me unafraid. It made it so I could walk the streets unafraid of any person or animal alive. That feelin' helps a man to take care of his family, to get up and leave the house on those days when he feels like he's all alone and he don't understand nothin'." Just then, Dad got one of those looks, like he didn't understand anything. The ocean wind blew straight into his face as he looked into mine. "Do you follow what I'm sayin' at all, George?"

"Sure I do, Dad." I found myself staring at the scars that zigged around his face like a tire tread. Up till then, I thought they were beautiful. "Boxing made you feel tough, right?"

He grabbed my shoulders. "Ya, but that's only half of it. Shit, that ain't one goddamn millionth of it. George, you got to hear me, right now. The trick is, you learn to take care of y'self, but save your head. It was important to me that you could take care of y'self, George."

I was taller than him, standing on that wall. I bent in a fighter's crouch, raised my fists in Dad's peekaboo style, went nose to flattened nose with him. "I know how to take care of myself." I smiled.

He grabbed me so quick and hard that my hands stayed pressed against my face, my elbows dug into my sides as he hugged. "Yes you do, son. I believe you learned your lessons good. That was one of the two things your old man had to give to you. Now we're gonna work on th' other, the one I didn't learn until way too late. I taught you how to fight. Now I'm gonna teach you how *not* to be a fighter, how to walk away."

It was a little confusing, after all I'd learned, but he told me that I'd understand it eventually. Not that it mattered—whatever Dad was teaching, I was studying. He was the smartest guy I ever knew, when you came right down to it. "But why is it too late?" I asked as he nudged me down off the wall. "Can't you just walk away now?"

He threw a couple of light jabs into my chest. He gave me one more smile—this was some kind of a big day for him with all that grinning—before getting back to business. "We'll see," he said. "Hit the road, young man." We finished the run home pushing hard, with me laying down three steps for every one of his.

Dad never got around to showing me much about not fighting. Unless being dead nineteen days later was his idea of walking away. I found him on the kitchen floor, his face against the linoleum, a puddle of drool stringing down from his mouth. It was dark, only 5:30 A.M. The time we'd normally be spending alone doing our road-work. So I sat down. Just sat there next to him on the linoleum for a while. Just the two of us.

For a second, I thought I might hit him, though.

I just didn't understand nothin'.

1

Groundwork

Easter Sunday afternoon Monty was lying on the couch in front of the TV. He was sleeping in front of one of those Jesus movies with a thousand different actors in it that he always sleeps through on a Sunday afternoon. First, he eats his weight at dinner, which isn't all that much, then he sacks out for a couple of hours. I sat next to him, by his feet, since he didn't take up more than half the length of the sofa, and Ma was in the kitchen doing the dishes. I got up to put my suit coat on.

"Where do you go, George?" Monty surprised me, opening his eyes a crack.

"No place. Go back to sleep."

He propped himself up on one elbow. "Every holiday, you put on your suit coat and sneak away, like if we have a Friday or a Monday off from school, George has to go someplace on Sunday to pay for it."

"I don't sneak. I just walk right out the door, and everybody who's awake knows about it."

"So where do you go?"

"Out."

"Is it any fun—out?"

"*Everything* doesn't have to be for fun, Monty."

"Then it's not fun, right? It couldn't be fun if you gotta wear a jacket for it. So why do you go?"

"Watch your movie, or go back to your nap."

"Can I come with you?"

I made a sucking-lemons face. "No."

He sat up, like he was going to come anyway. "Why not?" he said.

"Because you're a kid."

"I am not a kid."

"Monty, you're eleven years old, and you still take naps. That's about eight years later than when I stopped."

"George." Monty looked and sounded like I'd hurt his feelings. "You know that the doctor said I'm hyperactive, and that by the end of the week I get run-down."

"That's right, I did know that. I'm sorry. So, take the rest of your nappy now so you don't get too run-down."

Monty stood up and put his jacket on. He walked over and stood beside me, his head coming just above my shoulder. I stared down at him. He didn't move.

"Listen, if you just follow me saying stupid things, and spoil my day, I'm sending you home. And change that jacket—put on your good one."

Monty put on his blue blazer with the gold buttons. We went up to Ma, at the kitchen sink. "I'm going out, Ma," I said. She looked around me at grinning Monty. "He's coming with me," I said without a lot of enthusiasm.

She raised her eyebrows, smiled, almost laughed, nodded, and kissed us both. "Have a fine time, men," she said.

When we got downstairs, Monty asked, "How do you do that? All I have to do is go into the bathroom, and Ma says 'Where are you going, Monty?' 'What are you doing, Monty?'"

"Me and Ma understand each other. She trusts me. She pretty much knows all the time what I'm doing, and it's okay with her. But here's a tip: If you go out of the house in a suit coat, she cuts you a little more slack since you're probably not going to be jumping off roofs or hangin' with your boys down on the corner."

Monty waved his finger at me like "Hey, there's news you can use," as if my story were a trick story. That's why I have to be careful about what information I give him. "But I don't care if you go out in a tuxedo," I reminded him. "I'll want to know where your little butt is going." He sighed.

We waited for the bus in the bright sun, in our navy-blue jackets, light-blue pants, white shirts with white ties. It wasn't very hot out, but it started to seem it. The bus pulled up close to us on the curb, making it even hotter.

Monty put his hand on my arm as I was about to sit. "Remember, George, I get bus sick when I have my suit on," he said. I looked up at the ceiling as he climbed into the double bench first, to get the window seat. It was only a ten-minute ride anyway, out of our neighborhood, past the brick apartment houses, the few playgrounds, the cars on either side of the street jacked up with somebody underneath, or abandoned. A few corner stores with kids hanging out in front. It was the later, lazy part of Easter Sunday, and we only saw a few bonnets, baskets, families walking together but looking hotter and less happy than they had at church in the morning. The guys selling droopy flowers out of station wagons were pretty much out of business.

The bus pulled into a section of town where real flower shops seemed to be everywhere. There weren't a lot of houses around, but a lot of open space, a batch of four or five cemeteries. A big, wide intersection on a parkway, four corners, four florists.

"This is it," I told Monty as I stood up.

"This? This is where we're going? There's nothing here, George." I pointed at Mount Calvary Cemetery while he followed me down the stairs of the bus. "You sure know how to have fun, man," he said.

We crossed the street and walked in through the big front gate, past the square cement office. "They have maps in there," I said. "You can find anybody you want. They have a kind of celebrity tour. Some guys from the Revolution and the Civil War are over in section C. Ray Bolger, the guy who was the Scarecrow in *The Wizard of Oz*, is up on that hill there in D. Eugene O'Neill is in B."

"Who's Eugene O'Neill?" Monty said as we walked down the wide asphalt path.

"He was a great writer," I said.

"Oh ya," Monty said, not looking at me, trying to read the names on every stone we passed. "What did he write?"

"Well, I can't think of any of the titles right now. But they were great, they were big, and he's here."

Monty read the name of someone we knew from the old neighborhood, but it wasn't the same person. He suddenly stopped short, looking over at me.

"And who else is here, George?" He looked at me sideways.

"Come on, Monty. You're a kid, but you're not a dink. You know Dad's here."

Monty looked at the ground. "Ya, I know he is." He looked up and down the rows to his left and right, at the many piles of flowers that were left that day, at little flags stuck in the ground. The wrapper off of a peanut-butter egg tumbleweeded down the road.

"We don't have anything," he said.

"Don't worry about it."

"I was little the last time I came here. It was a long time ago, I don't remember it much."

I slapped him on the arm. "Come on," I told him. It had been a long time since he'd been there, probably three years. Ma doesn't care much for coming, and I like to come alone. So by the time I was ten and could travel pretty much everywhere the buses went, Ma mostly left it up to me.

We got to the top of the hill in section B. Turning off the main drive, we walked past the Robinsons, mother and father and three kids. They weren't in the ground, they were live people from the old neighborhood. They were the most religious people we knew, the whole family going

14

to church every day and all. They didn't even have a TV, which pretty much says it all, so Pat used to have to sneak over to all his friends' houses to watch. They didn't say anything when they passed us, just nodded and smiled enough so we wouldn't think they were hostile or anything.

We zigzagged between stones, some flat on the ground, some tall. There were a lot of angels, and a lot of war-memorial type things, but mostly plain rectangles. We came to the one. "Here we are," I said to Monty.

Monty stopped, like he was a little afraid, but mostly like he didn't know what he was supposed to do. I walked straight over, stepping around a newly planted lump of a grave. I stood in front of the stone, and Monty pulled up beside me.

"What's that?" Monty blurted, waving his finger madly at the inscription. Next to our father's name was our mother's, with her date of birth and a space for the day she's going to die. "I don't remember that being there."

"It's always been there, Monty," I said.

"Well let's get rid of it. Fill it with cement or something. I don't like it."

"We're not getting rid of it. It was Ma's choice. She wanted it there."

"I don't like it, George," he said, more angry.

He wasn't going to change his mind, so I steered him to something else. "What about the rest of the stone?" I said.

"Huh?"

"The other stuff, do you like it?" I walked right up and patted the headstone on top, rubbed its face. "I picked it out, you know."

"Ah, I don't think so, George."

"I wouldn't make something like this up. Ma had to go down to the monument maker, to take care of everything. I wasn't even as old as you are now. She said to me 'George'—she always called me Georgie before that, or Mr. Magoo—'George, I'm going to need a lot out of you now. You're the man.' You're the man, is what she told me. I told her that was okay with me, even though I was nervous because I wasn't sure what being the man was exactly all about, and Dad wasn't able to show me everything because . . . well, because he wasn't really *focused* during a lot of the time I knew him. I figured I knew enough, though."

Monty had wandered a bit, down the row to read other stones, head down like he wasn't paying attention.

"Are you listening to me?" I said.

"Ya," he said quietly.

"So then she says, 'George, what I have to do

now is a lonely job. Would you like to accompany me? It is all right if you don't.' I put on my coat and went with her in that hot smelly black Chevette with half a floor Dad left us. Remember the Chevette?"

"The Black Hole."

"Right. Anyway, she goes, 'What do you think?' when she had it narrowed down to a smooth, shiny black stone with a Celtic cross on top and this plain, rough gray one. The black one cost maybe ten times what this one cost, and I didn't think it was any finer. It looked too shiny, like a toy or the hood of a car. And that wasn't my dad, y'know?"

"*Our* dad," Monty said.

"That's what I meant. So I told her to get this one. She didn't even hesitate. She looked happy that I picked it, and told the man right away, picking that little rose engraving I liked too, out of a book with hundreds of designs. The only thing I didn't get the way I wanted it was, I didn't want Ma's name on there."

Monty had walked down the row one way and back the other, staying away and listening at the same time. Now he stood right in front of me with his hands on his hips. "Why didn't you pick one of those?" he said, pointing to the line of mausoleums running along the outer edge of the grounds. He

17

said it like he was blaming me for something.

"Come on, man, look at those mothers. Who could pay for something like that, you? It's like a house. If we could afford a house, Ma'd buy us a house. But I'll tell you what. I think if that's what I picked out, Ma would have tried to buy one."

Monty walked back and forth nervously. Suddenly he ran to one of the tall angel monuments nearby and stole some flowers from it. He came back and dropped them on the ground in front of our stone. "Why do you like to come here, George?" He was pacing again.

"I don't think anybody actually *likes* coming. . . ." I wasn't sure I was telling the truth.

"The Stiff Family Robinson *loves* to come here. They go to places like this all the time," he nearly yelled, pointing back toward where we'd seen the Robinsons, like he was mad at them now.

"Cut that out, Monty. You can't be yelling and saying stuff about people here."

"I want to go now, George. Can we?"

Monty was already walking down the path. I caught up to him, and we walked the asphalt road without talking until we were nearing the front gate. The sun was bright wherever we walked.

"Monty, you want to go see the Scarecrow?" I said from just back of his shoulder.

"Nope." He walked steadily.

"You want to talk about Dad?"

"Nope."

"Will you tell me when you do want to?"

He walked even faster. "Yup."

We crossed the wide intersection again and stood in the sun in front of the florist. "Maybe I'll just finish my nap next time, and you can go alone," Monty said while we waited for the bus.

"I'm sorry, Monty. Maybe it was too soon for this."

"Nope," he said, looking at me for the first time in a while. There was sweat on his upper lip, but he was looking hard.

"You want to take your jacket off?" I said.

"Yup."

"Take it off, then."

We both took our jackets off just before the bus pulled up and blew dirt and heat all over us again. We sat in a double seat, Monty at the window. He stared off. I knew what he was thinking about because I'd been there before. Though I'm not really a huggy kind of a guy, I put my arm around his shoulders.

"Listen," I said, "when we get home, you wanna fight?"

"Yo," he said.

He has all the *Rocky* movies on video.

19

2

Take the Body

"All right, lace 'em up, junior," I said as we walked down the back stairs. Actually, there were no laces since we fought with old hockey gloves, but we liked to use the fighting words to get ourselves fired up.

"You're not going to talk to me, are you, George? I mean, for once, can we just rumble without talking?"

When we got to the bottom of the three flights, we pulled the gloves out of our pile of stuff—goalie pads, football, basketball, rolls of tape—that we kept in the old dead freezer.

"Lesson number one—how many times do I have to repeat lesson number one?—do not concern yourself with what the other guy is doing. Focus. Focus. If my talking knocks you off your game, Monty, then some bad boy with a big right hand is gonna knock you on your butt. Understand?"

Monty slipped his gloves on, then smacked them together. "Ya, I understand. You're gonna yak at me."

"I'm gonna yak at you."

The lot behind the building was about big enough for three good-sized American cars. But it wasn't a parking lot. It may have been one at one time, because there were spots where the ground was paved with blacktop. But there were others where it was just dirt, or gravel, or a mix of everything, including concrete chunks. We roped off our ring using clothesline and long handles off push brooms donated by Nat, the superintendent. Because of the soft spots and the hard spots we had to work around, our ring wasn't exactly square. From a plane, it probably looked like a trapezoid. But it was useful because it was easy to whip it up and pull it down without Ma ever seeing it. No fight fan, Ma.

"So who you gonna be?" I asked Monty as I warmed up, shuffling my feet in the dirt.

"Julio Caesar Chavez," he said with a big grin, like he'd already whipped me.

"Can't be Chavez," I said.

"Why not?" He stood flatfooted in the middle of the ring.

I shadowboxed in a circle around him. "Because Chavez is a lightweight. And I'm gonna be Thomas Hearns. Hearns is a light-heavyweight. There just ain't no way a lightweight can go with a light-heavyweight."

As I figured, this threw Monty. Chavez is bad, and Monty had his heart set on him.

"Chavez could do it," he insisted, with his hands unwisely on his hips.

"Not even Chavez," I said. I stopped dancing, stood directly in front of him—*pop-pop*—and rapped him once on each side of his bony rib cage. That was his wake-up call. He raised his hands in front of his face and started bouncing.

"Lesson number one, Monty. Lesson number one: Focus." I started circling him again, but this time he followed me intently, duct-taped gloves framing his face. "You gotta pay attention to me, but *don't* pay attention to me, at the same time." I stepped in close to him again and gave him two more rib bangs before jumping back out of range. "And take the body, Monty. That's one of the most important things to learn. Take the body." I let him close in on me, then take a wild swing at my head. "I know you don't believe me now, Monty, but you will eventually. You gotta take the body. If you smack a person in the face, it makes that person want to fight. But if you hit him good in the gut, take the wind out of him, then that

22

person *doesn't* want to fight. And that"—I stopped backpedaling to wave my glove at him for emphasis—"is what you want."

Monty never broke stride as he came flying toward me, then past me. Red-faced, he wanted my head, but all he got was rope as he threw himself right out of the ring.

"You just won't believe me, I guess," I said as he sat on the ground looking down.

"Oh no, don't quit now," Buchanan called from the yard next door, where he didn't live. As soon as he heard the voice, Monty jumped to his feet and started tapping his gloves together. Buchanan—that was the only name anyone had ever called him, teachers included—jumped the short chain-link fence with Festus clinging to his shoulder. Festus was his weasly-faced ferret.

"Yo, blondie," Buchanan said as he got near my brother. "Why don't you let me have a pair of them gloves and I'll show you what a whippin' is about."

Monty turned to me for a second, but I didn't say anything. He had to do it himself. He understood, turned to Buchanan. "Say, I hear you. But I can do you better. How 'bout we have a tag team, me and my brother against you and yours." He pointed to Festus.

I laughed out loud, partly because I knew how

scared Monty really was. Buchanan was not your average eleven-year-old hard guy. He had been thrown out of Monty's class a year before for carrying a razor. Not the switchblade type, just one of the small flat kind they use to open cartons at the supermarket. Since then he just kind of mysteriously appears like a shadow in places where he's not wanted. Which is easy enough because he's not wanted anywhere.

"Shut up!" Buchanan yelled when I didn't stop laughing. Shut up. At me. This kid was only eleven years old. Granted, they were eleven hard ones, but I was thirteen.

"Listen here, little man," I said.

"Listen nothin'," he said. Festus had scrambled down and was rubbing his back against Monty's ankles. Monty crouched down and petted it with his gloves. Buchanan patted his own behind, the pocket where legend said his blade was supposed to be. "You don't want to mess with the Cannon"—that's what he called himself. "Now, I *know* you don't want to mess with the Cannon."

I dropped my gloves on the ground and walked toward him.

"Hey, Cannon," Monty said, growing bolder with every step *I* took. "Check it out, your brother is sniffing my butt." Festus was, in fact, nuzzling his way up there. Buchanan made a growling noise but didn't take his eyes off me. Monty kept on, "Yo, Festus, I mean Cannon—I can never get you guys straight—your brother is munching on something that looks a lot like dog squat." I didn't look to see if that one was for real.

When I reached him, I got right in Buchanan's face. He was a big kid, up to my eyes almost. He didn't blink. Monty stopped mouthing.

I dropped my voice down as low as it would go, which these days is pretty low. "That better be an Uzi in your pocket, if you're thinking about getting into it with *me*."

Everyone stayed stiff for a few long, sweaty seconds. Even Festus.

Cannon started walking backward. "Festus," he yelled, "get over here." The ferret wiggled his way back to his owner, shinnied him like a tree. Silently, Cannon pointed at Monty, staring. Then he hopped back over the fence, and he and Festus slunk away.

"Whoa, George. That was awesome, *awesome*," Monty said. I rubbed my eyes. They were dry from not blinking. Monty walked back and forth nervously, smacking together the gloves he was still wearing. "But you know, I really wanted to see you drop him. You should have KNOCKED him out." Monty slammed his gloves together hard when he said it, loud enough to grab my attention. When I looked into his face I saw that he was fighting tears. I turned my back and walked toward the ring, to give him some space.

"Monty, I didn't hit him because I didn't have to." I picked up my gloves where I had dropped them, then turned around. Monty was staring toward the fence where Buchanan had just vanished. "Understand? You don't do it if you don't have to. Monty . . ."

He slowly came back to the ring, looking back over his shoulder every few steps.

"Are we finished?" I asked him.

He looked away again. "Just wait. You'll see . . ."

"What?" I grabbed his shoulder and turned him toward me.

"Let's get to it," he said.

We got back in the ring. We started slowly like before, me circling him. I wanted to go easy because Monty looked a little grim, a little fuzzy around the eyes.

Then—*thump-thump-thump*—he stepped up and nailed me. Three times. Belly, belly, ribs. Then he jumped back. At first I was too stunned to move, so I just stood there.

Thump-thump-thump. So he did it to me again. Now he had focus.

26

3

Monty Got Soul

Monty plays the blues. I don't know for sure, of course, but I suspect that every time he's alone in the house, he plays air guitar in front of the full-length mirror inside our closet door for hours at a time. All I know for certain is that every time I come home and surprise him, that's how I find him.

And he never plays anything happy. It's always blues, blues-rock, that kind of stuff. He's never taking big windmill chops at his ax or jumping on top of amplifiers or wiggling his butt at the girls in the audience like any normal kid would. He always has his head thrown way back, his eyes closed, squinting like he's in horrible pain. The actual musician, the one on the record, makes the guitar sound like a human voice crying, while he and Monty sing together about all the brutal things some girl did to them and about not having any money.

27

"Can't you play air accordion or air fiddle just for once?" I yelled, shocking him from the doorway. "This is getting really depressing."

"Jeez, George," he yelled back, his ears turning red, fists at his sides. "Do you always have to scare me? Can't you just slam the front door when you come in or something?"

I walked over and flopped on the bed. "Why, what would you do then, straighten up and be normal before I make it down the hall?"

"I'm not being *not* normal. I only did it for a second. I was just goofin'."

I couldn't help laughing. I was looking at both sides of him while he stood with his back to the mirror trying to tell me that his performance was just a spontaneous thing. "Ya, right. You just happened to be walking by the closet and the door just happened to pop open and your Rolling Stones clothes just happened to fall out and land on your body." Monty was wearing black jeans that were tight for him, which is a tough thing with his Popsicle-stick legs. He had on a black T-shirt with the sleeves cut off, and I have to admit he looked pretty much like a real rock 'n' roller, with his bright-white arms hanging down like a pair of new sneaker laces. I never saw him wear the outfit out of the house.

"I felt like being comfortable, all right? There's nothing wrong with that."

"No, of course there isn't. But if you want to be a star, why bother aping records? Why don't you play your own guitar instead?" Monty had a guitar my mother bought him for his birthday last year. She had to be the only mother in history who was hot for her son to play guitar. She said it was a healthy outlet for Monty, to pursue his more spiritual side. He had some instruction books, and he did practice a lot, but the guitar was really an embarrassment to him. It was a folk guitar. And it was kid size. And it was red. Ma just didn't know any better.

"Leave me alone, George. I don't feel like playing anymore."

"Don't be like that, now. Here, I'll get it for you." All the time Monty would play for the mirror with nothing in his hands, his real guitar, the one that didn't fit his image, sat only a few feet away on a shelf in the closet, covered with sweaters. I pulled it down while Monty started taking off his black clothes.

"Here you go," I said as I held the guitar out to him.

He had the T-shirt off and was pulling a green-and-white rugby shirt over his head. He waved me

29

off without looking at me.

"Oh, don't be selfish, Monty. Let me hear you play."

He didn't answer.

"Okay," I said, "I'll be you, then." Monty used my mother's old wide patent-leather belt for a strap. I slung it over my shoulder. I stood for a few seconds with my feet wide apart, smiling at myself in the mirror; then I started. Jumping high in the air and in all directions, I played that guitar like I was going to kill it. I hacked at the strings as hard as I could without cutting my fingers, squeezing different spots on the neck without any idea what sounds it would make. I howled like a coyote.

Monty threw himself on the bed. "Cut it out, George," he said.

I ran right up to the mirror, putting my face to the glass like a rock star at the mike. I sang.

> "OOOOHHHHH
> *My name is Monty and I sing to my closet.*
> *I'm all screwed up and we don't know what*
> *caused it.*
> OOOOOOOOOHHHHHHHHHHH"

Monty lay on the bed on his back like a dead man, with *Mad* magazine covering his face. From under the magazine he moaned, "George, if you aren't the meanest guy in the world, then I'd hate to be the brother of the guy who is."

That only added fuel, as I laughed too hard to go on singing but continued to shriek and abuse the guitar.

"George," my mother's voice said from the doorway. Suddenly the little guitar around my neck weighed five hundred pounds and I was playing it naked in the middle of the street. "May I have a word with you out in the kitchen, please?"

I looked at her standing there in her raincoat. This had to be ten times worse than when I surprised Monty from that same spot. "Hi, Ma," I croaked. "How was work? Have you been standing there a long time? I never even heard you come in."

"No kidding," she said. "Get in the kitchen."

She went out ahead of me. Monty was peeking over the top of the magazine, but he hid his face again when I looked at him. When I started the long walk to go meet my mother, Monty started laughing. I stopped.

"Think this is funny, huh?" I challenged him.

"Oh no, I swear, I'm laughing at *Mad*. This is a really funny issue."

"Oh, right," I said. Then Ma yelled for me. As I was walking out the bedroom door, Monty was laughing harder than before.

31

"This might be the funniest *Mad* of all time," he said.

When I reached the kitchen finally, my mother was sitting at the table tapping her fingers. Up and down they went, drumming in perfect step, pinky, ring, middle, index, pinky, ring, middle, index. Her long nails on the end of her long fingers drove the volume up to a scary level.

"Want to split a ginger ale?" I said.

"Sit down, George. Son, is there something wrong with you that I should know about?"

I thought about it. Was this a trap, or was she worried about me? "No," I said. "Not that I know of."

"Is it the rain, perhaps, that makes you a little nutty?"

"I don't feel nutty. No, the rain's okay."

"So everything's fine with you then, is it, George?"

"Ya. Ya, Ma I feel pretty good, thanks." I had forgotten why we were there.

"Well then you should be very proud of yourself. That was one of the unkindest displays I have ever seen."

I was right—it was a trap. I wished she would brain me with the guitar instead of doing the "how rotten is George" thing. She was great at it, and even if I saw it coming, it scored and it hurt for a week.

"Ma, I was only playing—"

"Is that how you play? What am I going to have to do, George, quit my job so that I can be here all the time to monitor the psychological torture you call play?"

"No" was all I said. The things I did were always a lot funnier when I did them than when she described them back to me, and she always got me seeing it her way before I could get her to see it mine.

"I'm very disappointed in you, George. I count on you to be pretty responsible around here, to be the man, and when you let me down it's twice as bad. Something's going to have to be done about this. You know the score here. This guitar playing is a good thing for Monty. It's good for everybody. I cannot have you intimidating it out of him. Your brother is an extremely sensitive boy, you know that. He's probably sitting in that room right now crying because of your cruelty, the poor little guy."

When it was all over and I was allowed to slither back to my room, the poor little sensitive guy was standing in front of the mirror again with the guitar on. Right when I walked in, he sang.

> "Ya, my name is Georgie, I was killed by my
>   mother,
> Then she gave all my stuff to my brother.
> Doo wah."

He was killing himself laughing before he got to the end. His song was better than mine too, because he had a tune that he stole from a real song, and he played the notes right.

"You know, you're right, George," he said. "I should sing more happy songs. This is fun." It made me feel a little better that Monty was getting more pleasure out of my getting chewed out than I got out of acting up in the first place.

"Nice song, man."

"That's it, nice song?" I had accidentally insulted his work by not getting pissed off. "You're not going to attack me or anything?"

"Nah, I'm just not into it right now. It was a great song, though. Maybe I'll beat on you later if I think of it." I sat on the army-green, fake-leather love seat that we used to pile our clothes on. Monty came over and sat next to me, wearing the guitar. He frowned.

"What happened? You didn't really get hit, did you?" He was concerned, as if he had forgotten how it all started in the first place.

34

"Worse. I wish I got hit."

"Grounded?"

"Worse."

"She making you visit Grandma?"

"Shut up already. I'll tell you. I have to learn 'Happy Birthday' on . . . that." I smacked the guitar, making it ring. "I have to learn the stupid song in a week and then I have to play it and . . . SING it to you. . . ."

"ON MY BIRTHDAY!" Monty broke in. His birthday was one week away. He threw himself on the floor in front of me and lay on his back laughing, strumming, and singing. "Ma is the best," he said. "She's just the best. I feel like it's my birthday right now." Suddenly he stopped. He stayed motionless on the floor, looking up as if his life were passing before his eyes. I looked back down at him, my knees only a few inches away from his bony little chest.

"You're not going to kill me, are you, George?"

"Nope," I said. He climbed back up beside me.

"Are you okay?" he said. "You don't look so good."

"There's nothing wrong with me."

"Listen, George, if you want, you don't have to sing to me. I'll just tell Ma I don't want you to."

"No, I don't want you to do that. I should have

to do it. Ma's right. There's something wrong with me. I should be the guy taking care of you, but I torture you."

Monty looked at me like he didn't understand. Then he looked away and strummed chords quietly. "I know how to play 'Happy Birthday,'" he said. "You want me to show you?"

"Funny you should mention that," I said. "That's part of the deal."

We spent the rest of the afternoon in the room together while Monty tried to show me everything he knew about the guitar and music in general. He made "Happy Birthday" as simple for me as he could, breaking it down into three easy chords and showing me how to position my fingers to play them. Then he played the song for me *his* way. It sounded like something a blind guy would play on the subway.

"Tell me something, Monty," I said as I tried to imitate his playing. "Why do you play blues all the time? You got women and money troubles I don't know about?"

"Uh-uh. But I don't find too many songs about stuff that bothers me, so I just imagine that I have women and money problems. Then when I sing 'em away, the other stuff kind of goes along with them. It feels good—it's like when stuff gets out of control and I want to scream or run or whack somebody, somehow this blows off some of that steam. I don't know how it works, really."

I played "Happy Birthday" once all the way through without mistakes. Then I gave Monty back the guitar. "Now show me that twelve-bar blues thing again," I said.

He grabbed the guitar, threw his head back, and squinted. I copied him.

4

Men at Work

Because we live in an old building with a lot of apartments full of people who don't have much money, things break all the time. Some months it seems like every person who walks through the door has a tool belt hanging around his waist. But the guy who did most of the fixing around the place never wore a tool belt. His name was Nat, and he was the superintendent.

Nat was a chubby guy with one tooth and, I think, one T-shirt, with beige stains under the arms. He was always wearing the shirt except when we would go to his office down in the boiler room and find it hanging over a pipe to dry. Nat would be sitting at his desk without a shirt, watching game shows on a small TV he took out of the trash. He said the shirt was hanging because he washed it, but it didn't smell that way. The reason he didn't wear a tool belt was because he used only two things to do his work. "This is for putting things together," he said, holding up a roll of duct tape, "and this is for taking things apart." He held up a hammer.

I liked Nat because he acted like he didn't know we were kids, and was always throwing odd jobs our way.

Usually, the kind of work Nat gave us was stuff like washing windows or hauling trash or some other little detail that was actually part of *his* job, but he didn't feel like doing it so he sat on the steps eating a bag of cheese curls and watching us do it. That was fine with us, because we *wanted* to work. It was more than just the peanuts Nat paid us, it was training. The kind of people who need Monty and me to do stuff for them are the kind of people *we'll* never be. People who can't take care of themselves. That's something I learned a long time ago, and it's my job to make sure that Monty learns it as well.

So when Nat said he had a furniture-moving job for us, we were pumped because there's money in that *and* it's real man's work.

"Well, I don't know that y'all are prepared for this particular assignment," Nat said as he painted the fire escape with black Rust-Oleum.

"What?" I said. "Remember the time I lowered

39

Monty into the sewer by his ankles when you lost all the keys to the building?"

"Hee-hoo." Nat laughed his "good ol' boy Carolina crow," as he called it.

"Ya," Monty said. "Remember that? Remember how I cut my head on those scummy old sewer bricks and it got all infected?"

"Hee-hoo," Nat laughed.

"Hee-hoo," Monty followed.

"Ya, Nat, and remember that time when it was one hundred and eleven degrees in July and we mixed cement for you all day so you could patch all the cracks in the foundation? Remember how Monty passed out and he wouldn't wake up until I waved ammonia under his nose? He got right back to work, though, didn't he? We finished the job— even after *you* quit—didn't we?"

Nat laughed louder and louder as I made my pitch. Monty laughed with him, because Monty always laughed with Nat.

"All right, Mr. George, all right," Nat said, shaking his head as he shook up a new spray can. "What we gotta do is to haul a bunch of junk outta somebody's house for a yard sale. Be on the sidewalk Saturday at eight A.M. Don't you boys be late now, or ol' Nat goes alone."

Since it was going to be hard work, we knew

ol' Nat wouldn't be going alone. But we were ten minutes early anyway. The three of us walked the half mile to the house where we'd be working. It was right off the main street, near the elevated tracks they didn't use anymore. Monty and I walked by the place every day on the way to school, and the windows on the first floor were all boarded up. I never figured anybody lived there. Just as we turned the corner of the street, Nat, who was unusually quiet during the walk, said, "Boys, ever seen *The Elephant Man?*"

"No," Monty said. "Why, you taking us to the movies?"

Nat started to laugh, but I could see he didn't mean it. "Ya," he said quietly. "I'm sorta takin' you-all to the movies."

When we arrived, we found stuff already on the lawn. There were a couple of rolled-up rugs on one side of the path and three rickety brown kitchen chairs on the other side. Up on the porch there was a ratty rattan fan-back chair. The front door was open, so we walked in.

Just inside, four steps up the staircase, a love seat stood on end, wedged in tight between the wall and the banister.

"This thing stinks," Monty said.

"It sure do," Nat said.

"Hi, guys," a muddy, muffled voice said from the other side of the couch. "I'm Frank," he said. He was tough to understand, like he had his mouth pressed up against the seat cushion.

I could feel my face turning red, I don't really know why, when I said "Hi" back. Monty didn't say anything. We both looked to Nat. "Hey, Frankie-boy," Nat said. "I brung 'em."

"You're a good man, Nat," Frank said. Then he poked his head up over the top of the love seat.

It was the biggest head I ever saw. And his skin was all warty. But that wasn't the biggest thing. Frank's tongue was all swollen like nothing I ever saw before. It was growing way out, straight ahead and side to side as if he had a potato hanging from his mouth. When he talked it didn't move, but his lips opened and closed around it. The whole hallway smelled strong, a little like fish and a little like ammonia. I was sure that I was staring, but I couldn't stop. I only hoped I didn't look like Monty, who was zombified. I turned again to look at Nat behind me, but he'd already slithered off.

"Boy, you guys showed up at just the right time," Frank said. "I think that if you both just pull the bottom out, it'll slide right out of here." We were happy to go to work. Without even answering him, Monty and I both yanked as hard as we could, and the love seat came thumping down those last four steps. We hadn't even given Frank a chance to grab the other end—we just dragged it right out to the porch, down the stairs, all the way out onto the lawn. As soon as we dropped the couch, Monty whispered, "I say we pull a Nat and book on out of here." I thought about it, but I just shook my head.

Frank followed us out. "Jeez, Nat was right, you guys are animals," he said. "I'm sorry. I didn't mean that the way it sounded."

"That's okay," I said. Monty hung behind me. When we saw Frank's whole body, we were surprised all over again. He limped badly, basically dragging one of his legs. And he had one small arm. It stayed bent all the time, and the hand was dead and squishy-looking, like it couldn't do anything. It was a Tyrannosaurus Rex arm is what it was. "Can I ask you something?" I said.

"Fire away, young man," he said. I think he smiled. He was so cheerful, it made me mad for a second.

"Did you bring all this stuff down here by yourself?" I asked him without sounding too surprised.

"Well yes, I was up early this morning and I wanted to do what I could, so . . ." He shrugged, and the T. Rex hand wiggled back and forth. "Listen," he said. "You want to come up and look the job over?"

We followed Frank up the stairs, where yellow wallpaper with softball-size roses was rolling down off the walls. The exposed plaster was full of holes and had the smell of something living behind it. Inside the apartment, sticks of old veneer-and-particle-board furniture were placed here and there; pictures of clowns and cats hung in every room. Some of the windows were poked out, and I noticed that there was no phone and no sign of any live electrical appliances except an ancient Frigidaire, the fat kind with the rounded edges. And I wasn't about to open that to see if it was plugged in. The place sure felt like a condemned building.

Frank pointed out what was going outside for the sale and what wasn't. There was no way to tell how he made his choices. It was all crap. Every knickknack, every useless end table, every last nasty box that made our eyes sting with whatever that odor was. It was the kind of stuff Monty and I were always cleaning out of people's garages and basements and leaving on the sidewalk for the trashmen. I knew right away that nobody would buy any of this stuff. "Is this going?" Monty said in a rush, picking up a purple velour ottoman.

"Yes, it is," Frank said. Monty scooped it up and whisked it down the stairs. Frank turned to me. "You want something? I have instant coffee. Stove works." He said it like an apology.

"That would be nice," I said. As he went to make it, I took a stack of *People* magazines, tied with twine, downstairs. "I've got every issue," he called after me, really proud. "Right from the first." They were the only magazines I found— maybe forty of them—so I don't really think he did have every issue.

When I got outside, I looked all around for what I already suspected. Monty had pulled a Nat on me.

Frank came hobbling into view, balancing three coffees on his good arm. Like a waiter, only without a tray. "So, how do you know Nat?" I said as I took my cup. Frank was totally unfazed that I was the only one left.

"He's my friend," Frank said. "I met him at the shelter a long time ago, before he got successful. He still comes by sometimes, though, even though I move around a lot. He finds me. . . . He's my friend." He used the same tone he had when he mentioned the *People* magazines.

So we did the job together, me and Frank. He was slow, but he worked like a mule. With his good hand he helped me balance the kitchen table. He hauled down the cinder blocks that were the base of his coffee table and the frame of his bed. But mostly he brought me coffee. He didn't seem to smell anymore after a while. When I finished, I sat with Frank, observing as nobody came close to buying anything. Finally, a dirtier-looking guy than Nat came up with a buck for the *Peoples*, and that was it for me. I told Frank I had to go and shook his little hand. He paid me in returnable bottles and cans. I took them.

I found Monty on our front steps. He looked scared when he saw me. My free hand was balled in a fist, and with the other I slung the green bag of returnables right at him.

"There's our money," I said. I jabbed my finger in his face. "We do not run. Do you understand me? You're never going to run again. You won't be afraid of anything or anybody. . . ."

"I'm not afraid," he said weakly.

"I'm going to teach you. You can't run anymore."

Monty sighed. He tried to sound like he was bored with me, but he was terrified. "What's it, time for a lesson now, George? We going out back for a lesson?"

I brushed by him on my way into the house,

without looking at his face. "Monty, I can't take you out back when I'm angry. If we go now, I'll kill you. You missed your damn lesson today. I can't show you anything about toughness the way that guy could have. Want to see somebody tough? Want to see a guy who can take care of himself? Go back to Frank's. Now stay out of my face."

He didn't go back, but he did stay out of my face for the rest of the weekend. I don't know why, but this really ate at me, and Monty knew it. We didn't even talk again until Monday morning as we walked to school. I looked down Frank's street. As far as I could tell, everything we had moved was sitting out on the curb for the trashmen. Nobody bought it. In two days, nobody dragged it back in, nobody walked off with it. Monty deliberately avoided looking down the street until I grabbed him by the shoulders and pointed him that way.

He looked at the stuff. I locked my stare on him, making sure he didn't look away. His eyes went glassy, until finally he said, "I got it, George," then met my stare with his.

We nodded at each other and went on to school.

5

The Head

It wasn't that Monty didn't care about people like Frank, people who weren't quite complete packages. The thing really was that he felt *too* much. He always had this knack for befriending all kinds, from the cement-head football kids to the genius kids nobody understands to the kids who don't bathe. He'd sit and talk to the gargoyles outside the library if they'd only nod every once in a while. But there was one friend he had who I had trouble understanding. The kid was only around for six months, so I never got the chance to completely figure him out. Monty liked him right away, and that was a pretty hard thing for everybody else.

I don't know what it was, either. His name was Fred. "Fred the Head" was what everybody called him. He had a head shaped like an eggplant, with the narrow end at the top, and as far as I can tell, that was people's main problem with him, because he wasn't a bad kid at all. The bones over his eyes were caved in around the outside edges and his ears were small stumpy things. Every time I ever saw him, he had a big lump of hair sticking up from the back of his head like he'd slept funny on it.

One time when I was walking home from school, I stopped into the superette and Fred walked up to the counter. I wasn't there with him—we just happened to be there at the same time. The guy who worked there, a guy with only three front teeth and none along either side of his mouth, said to Fred, "You was a forceps baby, huh, kid?" and laughed like it was a joke they were going to share together. Fred was a smart kid and must have known what the guy meant, but he looked down at his feet and pretended not to hear. He did a lot of that.

Monty found the Head fascinating. From the minute his family moved into the Petersons' house four doors down, Monty was over there checking it out. I think at first it might have been because they showed up in a cab. And then the cab stayed and they went everywhere in it because Fred's father, who was also named Fred but who my mother called "The Willies" because she said he gave her the willies, drove a cab for work. But after that wore off, he kept being Fred's friend because the kid sparked Monty's overdeveloped Dedication thing. Monty adopted him.

Monty was reading the sports page on the floor in front of the TV one afternoon. "Why do you hang around with that zeroid all the time, Monty?" I asked him while I stared out the window at the Head taking his cat for a walk in the pouring rain. On a leash.

"Because he's my friend."

"So what?" I said. "You have lots of friends. Normal friends."

"You never said *that* before. You say all my friends are *Batman* characters."

"Ya, but this guy is like, king geek. Nobody hangs with the Head, Monty. I mean, nobody. Except you, of course. I'm not trying to be mean or anything, it's just that I think it's something you should know."

"I know." He looked up from his paper. "But even you, George? You really don't like Fred either?"

He has a way of asking me questions real innocently that makes me feel like some kind of bum before I even answer.

"I don't *not* like him," I said. I turned to look out the window again, over the back of the sofa.

"But look at the guy. Monty, come over here and look at this."

Monty climbed up on the sofa beside me. The two of us watched through the rain as Fred the Head stood in the park across the street with no coat on. It was late October and it was almost dark, and he stood there doing nothing, staring at his bony cat while the cat sat on the ground and stared back, each one just waiting for the other to do something.

"See?" I said.

Monty went back to the floor, crawling straight over the coffee table to get there. "So what?" he said.

"So something's just not right about him, that's what. Every time I see him, practically, he's being bizarre. I just don't see . . .."

"Well, I like him," Monty snapped. "I like him just because I like him. And you know what else?" He hopped to his feet and looked at me sideways, turning his head so far that I could see only one eye. "I'm going outside." He walked right out the door without putting his coat on.

I turned toward the street one more time and watched my brother walk up to the Head and the cat. Monty said a quick hi, the Head did too, and then they stood with their hands in their pockets.

The cat got up at first when Monty showed up, then sat back down when he realized they weren't going anywhere.

They were making me shiver just watching them until the cat made the first sensible move and they followed, back to the Head's place. That was the first time Monty ever went into that house. And since he was the only friend anyone in that family had, he was most likely the only other human to go inside the whole six months they lived there.

"So how was it?" I asked when he came back a half hour later. "You kids have a nice little oddball tea party?"

"Mr. Rafkin is the meanest man I ever saw" was all he could say. Fred's father was in charge of Fred and his sister, Mary B., by himself. There was no mother around and the kids never said anything about her. Ma said the Willies probably drank her. She was always saying drinking things about him, though I don't know how she knew anything about him since he was so quiet and spooky. Anyway, he took care of the kids by himself, but he didn't seem to like the job very much.

"You know how everybody calls Mary B. 'Herbie'?" Monty said. "Well you know where it started? Her father made it up. He called her

Herbie a million times while I was there. He told her, 'Herbie, it's just a goddamn shame you weren't a boy like I wanted you to be, because then it wouldn't be so bad that you're so ugly. And you could have been the son I never had.'"

"Wow," I said. "That's cold-blooded."

"That's nothing," Monty said. "He throws schoolbooks in the toilet, he puts his hand into the goldfish bowl and chases the fish around until they die, and if he catches the kids feeding the cat, he slaps the kid and cat both."

From the kitchen Ma heard Monty talking. She came stomping in. "Monty, do I hear you talking about the Willies? I told you, I don't want you going over there. That man drinks."

"Well so do you," Monty said before I could stop him.

"It's not the same thing," she barked. Even mentioning the Willies made her a little crazy. Comparing her to him was like poking her in the eye.

"I'm sorry," Monty said. "But Fred is my friend. Nobody else goes over there, so it would be nice if I could."

"Well you can't," she said. There was no more talk about it.

The next morning when we left for school,

Fred the Head was waiting on the steps with his sister. She did have the biggest teeth I had ever seen on a nine-year-old. Fred was all excited to offer us a ride to school. Monty looked at me and we both shrugged at the same time. "She didn't say anything about cars," I said. So we accepted. The thought of riding with Fred's father was no thrill, but the chauffeur deal had a kind of slickness about it.

The entire ride would only take five minutes, and when we had been driving for about two, Fred knocked on the Plexiglas that separated the front and back seats.

"Father," he said like a mouse. Monty and I looked at each other. We'd never heard anyone call their father "Father." The Willies didn't answer.

"Father," Fred said in a louder squeak.

"I heard you the first time," he said as if it made him sick to even speak.

"I need you to sign this," Fred said, stuffing his report card through the money slot. Right away I thought "Oh no, lousy grades. I'm going to see a kid butchered right before my eyes. Why else would he wait until now for this?" But that wasn't it at all. The Head was a smart kid. Monty smiled and leaned toward me. "Straight A's," he whis-

54

pered like it was *his* son he was bragging on. But the kid seemed worried. He and Mary B. looked at each other nervously.

The Willies looked at the card and drove at the same time. We peeked over the back of the seat to see his reaction. It would be nice to see the Head enjoy a bit of triumph.

But in the rearview mirror we saw his father make a disgusted face. He didn't say anything, just hit the accelerator and rolled down his window. In a whiff, that perfect report card was gone, flying in the opposite direction as fast as we were driving. We all turned to watch it disappear as Fred's father spoke.

"I told you this before. No son of mine is going to be a fag bookworm."

Fred didn't answer him, just sucked it up like it was routine. We all settled back down onto the seat, and Mary B. whispered to me, "None of our teachers ever get to see our report cards again after they give them to us."

Suddenly I noticed Monty was all red, like the Willies had done something to *him*. He rose up on his knees and stared again into the rearview mirror. "I just don't understand any of this," he said, so that anyone could hear him.

"Shut up and sit down," the Willies said.

Monty stood. He hopped up and pressed his face against the partition, flattening his tongue and making a pig nose for the Willies to see.

The Willies yanked on the wheel and screeched the brakes, setting off a blast of horns as he banged to the curb. We were all still rolling all over the floor when he screamed, "Get the fuck out."

None of us said a thing as we piled out, three blocks from school. Before I could stop him, Monty stuffed a dollar through the front window. The Willies nearly tore his arm off as he peeled away.

I held my head in my hands, thrilled to see the cab hauling down the street rather than the Willies killing a twelve-year-old. Monty threw his arm around Fred's shoulders and started walking him the rest of the way, thinking he'd done great. He had no idea how close he'd come. So much, he didn't know yet.

Forbidden Archie's

"I got us a job," Monty said as I strolled in from delivering my papers a half hour late. It was one of those holy days where our puny little school had the day off and the rest of the universe had to keep spinning as usual.

"You?" I said as I looked him up and down. He stood there smiling in a thick, baggy gray sweatsuit and Seattle Mariners baseball cap pulled so low over his ears that he looked like a poster kid for something. "You actually got up, got out, and got us a paying job?"

He grabbed my sweats off the chair and threw them at me. "You know it, brother. Get into your grubbies."

"What do we have to do? Where is it?" Not that it really mattered. I was already pulling my pants off.

"A little grunt work, that's all. As for the

where, you just come with me. It's a surprise." Monty left while I finished dressing. When I walked into the kitchen, he was sucking down the last of his raw-egg drink. The boxing movies again.

"One of these days I'm gonna walk in while you're doing that, and I swear, I'm gonna blow chunks right there."

Monty laughed at me. "Well, you drink coffee all the time. At least eggs are protein. Coffee has formaldehyde in it."

"That's decaf. I don't do decaf, buster."

"A very convincing argument for your health, Master George," Ma said as she strolled into the kitchen. She had a five-pound stack of folders under her arm. "I thought we were going to cut out that coffee business, George."

I pretended I didn't hear as I poured a splash of cream, acting very concerned about my brother. "Ma, were you aware that Monty was eating raw things again? What are we gonna do about this situation?"

"George?" She was drumming her fingers on the table, which was impossible to ignore.

"Ma, I thought about it. And I realized that I could stop anytime I want. It's just that I don't want to."

What I was saying made perfect sense to me,

but Ma didn't seem to take any comfort in that. Monty knew it right off too, stifling a laugh before Ma marched over and peeled my fingers from around the mug. "*Now* you want to, George." She sat at the table with my coffee and started gulping while she whipped through her files. "Honestly, George, I'm surprised at that kind of wise-guy stuff, coming from you."

"Go easy on him, Ma," Monty jumped in. "He never makes any sense before his first cup."

She raised her head slowly and glared at Monty. "As for you, Conan the Barbarian, salmonella is going to be a treat compared to what I'll do if I catch you ingesting any more uncooked food."

Monty pulled the bill of his cap way down over his eyes and started walking backward toward the door. "Gotta go to work, Ma," he said, waving me on.

"You boys have work? Where are you going? Do you want a ride?"

Monty was already on his way down the stairs. "Nah," he said. "Walking distance. Good for us."

I stopped at the door, shrugged, and smiled lamely at Ma before leaving. Monty was right—without the coffee I was a feeb.

Monty insisted it was a surprise, that I had to just follow him and he'd take me to the place. It was a small business moving into the neighborhood, and the owner needed some cheap underage labor to help him move in. The owner was the kind of guy who was our bread and butter.

"Pretty lucky for us he decided to move in on All Saints' Day, while all the other cheap underage souls have to be in school, huh, George?"

"Ya, it helps when you're the only game in town." We were walking by Cassidy's, about a block from our house. Cassidy's is a variety store that's no bigger than maybe twice the size of my bathroom at home. But he does have variety, from Chee-tos to jewelry to fat black cigars to Sony Walkmans to naked girlie air fresheners. There's really not even any room for fat old Cassidy in his own store, which is why he sits on a folding chair out front all day.

"Mornin' boys, how come you're not in school today?" Cassidy yelled, even though we were passing two feet away from him.

"Holy day." I jumped to answer before Monty did. The rule around town was that, like a PG-13 movie, you were not allowed to have any contact with Cassidy unless you were old enough or were accompanied by a parent or legal guardian.

"Oh ya, All Saints' Day, right?" Every word sounded like a cough. "You young saints gonna pray for my soul?"

"You gotta *have* one first," Monty blurted.

I gave Monty a little shoulder shove. "Come on, let's go."

"Hey, Fat City, whatcha got there?" Monty leaned around me and pointed at something snuffling behind Cassidy's big shoes.

"Thought you'd never ask," he said. He reached down and pulled out an animal that looked like a chubby Scottie dog. "This is a Vietnamese potbellied pig. It cost a thousand bucks. You want to touch it?" He put the little black beast into his lap and waved us over, "Come on."

Monty took a step toward him. This time I pushed him for real. "Get going," I said. Then I looked back at Cassidy. "You're gonna go broke eating those," I yelled.

"Hah," Monty said. "Good one, George."

"Hah nothing, where are we going?"

"A few blocks. Relax, will ya?"

"And how did you find this guy with the jobs? What kind of business are we talking about, anyway?" As we drifted into the badder streets, I got more curious.

"I just ran into him, that's all. Total coincidence. As for his business, you'll like it—it's a sports business."

"No lie? We're gonna load up a new sporting

61

goods store? Any freebies involved? New pair of cross trainers, maybe?"

"It's not exactly a store, George. But don't worry, it's better."

We walked all the way down Broadway to where the wrecking ball was swinging out a whole neighborhood full of houses where nobody was supposed to live but all Nat's friends probably did. I pictured Frank clutching his jar of Taster's Choice while the big steel ball swooped through his kitchen. We took a right down Lamartine, where the dead el tracks hang over everything and it's nighttime pretty much all the time.

"All right, Monty, this is enough. Where the hell are we going?"

He smiled and pointed across the street, to 615 Lamartine, an old brewery warehouse that was now just an empty block of yellow bricks next to a brake-pad factory.

"The warehouse?" I said.

Monty didn't even notice me. "He's here!" he yelled, and ran over to a U-Haul step van parked out front. When I caught up, Monty was standing there marveling at the stuff jammed in the back of the open truck: two fifty-pound and two seventy-five-pound heavy bags, treadmill, speedbags, weights, dozens of red gloves, tin buckets, miles of bandages. And a big white sign standing on one end. In green lettering it read "ARCHIE'S GYM, Est. 1969."

"Georgie." Archie's croakie voice called from the front stairs.

"Yo, Uncle Arch," Monty yelled, and ran to exchange forearm smashes with Archie. I stayed at the truck, staring at my uncle's boxing stuff, listening to his old familiar voice. Before I could catch my breath, his giant hands were hanging on my shoulders.

"Georgie," he said again, sadder and happier than the first time. I turned around. "Goddamn it, Georgie, you look so much like your old man I can hardly look at you."

"I can hardly look at you, too." I looked at my feet instead. Archie reached out and lifted my chin up with his fist. That was the natural shape of his hand now, a fist.

"I'm sorry to be foolin' you this way, George," Archie said.

"Foolin' him like what?" Monty asked, punching Archie in his big-lady tattoo and smiling dumbly.

"Listen, Monty, how 'bout haulin' some gear upstairs for me, while I talk to your brother for a minute?" Monty hopped right up on the truck and started attacking one of the small heavy bags. He punched it about twenty times, raising a little resin cloud, then wrestled it down to the street and up the stairs. It would take him a while, but both Archie and I knew he wouldn't be back till he got it up there by himself.

I sat on the truck's step and Archie joined me.

"I knew you wouldn't come if you knew it was me, Georgie, 'cause you're such a tightass. But I mean that good. You're a good man, George, and I know that if your ma doesn't want you doin' somethin', then you ain't doin' it. An' I know you take A-one care of that brother of yours too. Don't ask me, I just know."

It was hard for me to sit next to Archie while he talked like that, so I climbed into the truck with the stuff. I tapped lightly at a leather punching bag. "Well, if you know all that, then why am I here?"

He continued to talk out toward the street. About the only things moving out there were delivery trucks that sounded like all their bolts were loose when they hit the exposed cobblestones. "I always said you were a fine boy, Georgie. Since you were this big." He held up a pinky shaped like a letter C. "I always said, there goes a fine boy. I wish he was my son. And I ain't just blowin' smoke—you could ask your mother. That's one thing she has to say for me."

I don't know if Archie stopped talking or if the three trucks in a row drowned him out. Either way, I stopped hearing anything. The trucks passed and Archie sat quiet.

"Uncle Archie? Ah, I don't want to be a wise guy, but is that it? I mean, it feels good, what you're saying, 'cause a guy doesn't hear that kind of thing too often, but does it answer my question? Like, why . . . ?" I stopped punching the bag and leaned on it.

"Your dad was my only brother. You're his son. Monty's his son. I didn't die. The way you look after Monty, that's what I did, for thirty-five years." Monty came huffing down the stairs. As he neared, Archie's voice got smaller. "I got nobody. I understand how your ma feels, but . . . I didn't die. I got nobody. . . ."

Monty leaped onto Archie, grabbing him around his large head with its white crew cut. With Monty tugging at him, Archie turned his bull neck so he could look at me, to see what I was going to do. He knew I wasn't supposed to be there. There were only two times Ma felt she had to use the word "forbid" with me: She had forbidden me to bring home the girl with the black nail polish and the crucifix nose ring; and she had forbidden me to hang around Archie's Gym. Even when I told her I had no interest in going there, she still snapped, "I forbid it," like she knew that someday I might want to.

I was thinking while Archie stared at me with those foggy-looking eyes, over that pineapple nose. I was thinking that I'm not the only one who looks like my dad. Archie looks like him too, only my dad never got old, like Archie did. This wouldn't exactly be *hanging around* Archie's, is what I was thinking. It's business.

"Tell me something," I said as I dragged the leather bag to the edge of the U-Haul and pointed for somebody to grab the other end. "How did you two get together in the first place?"

"Yellow Pages," Monty blurted as he took the other end and we started working.

"Is that right?" I smiled. "Who called who?"

"I did," Monty and Archie said together. I had to laugh.

Archie balanced a box of gloves, clocks, and a bell on his head as he led us to the second-floor gym. "All right, George, listen, I know you guys do this kind of grunt work, so when I knew I was moving to this neighborhood, I called. Monty there answered. Loading the truck on the other end was no problem—all I had to do was crack open a bottle of Wild Turkey 101 and I had more workers than you could shake a stick at. Problem is, they're the kind of guys you might need to shake a stick at. And I didn't want to start bringing that stuff up here to the new place. That's part of why I'm here. I want a quiet place, a nice place."

Monty was silent the whole time Archie talked. But he worked like a bigfoot truck. Up and down and up and down he went, right along with us bigger guys, sometimes carrying nearly his own weight. Seemed Monty'd found some strength somewhere that even I hadn't noticed before. And he was about as happy as I had ever seen him while working. Everything we touched had the same smell on it—sweat and resin and mold. And blood and balls, Archie said. "That's the fighter smell, boys," he said when he noticed Monty taking it in deep for the tenth time. "That's what a fighting gym smells like, so that's what an honest fighter smells like because an honest fighter spends all his time in the gym."

When we had all the equipment up, I lay flat on my back in the middle of the big room. Even though it was on the second floor, it was nothing more than the dark musty cellar in our building, times ten. Except one whole wall was a mirror, because a dance studio had leased the place before. Archie said it only lasted three weeks.

"This place is *super*, Uncle Archie," Monty said as he furiously duked it out with his reflection.

Archie laughed, a little embarrassed. "Thanks, son." Then he sat on the floor by me. It was hard because none of his joints worked too well. "Time to talk business, Mr. George?"

I nodded. "Well, this was two hours, two men, pretty backbreaking stuff. Twenty-five dollars."

Archie rubbed his fist back and forth across his spongy nose. "Wow, you are tough. Ain't there a discount for family?"

"I'm sorry, no."

"I was thinking more like fifteen. It weren't really all that hard, after all. And your brother there had himself one fine time of it." Monty was wobbling under the weight of a pair of dumbbells. He dropped them to the floor with a loud clink, then pinched his biceps for the mirror.

"Twenty," I said. "And don't try to get me any lower or we'll put it all back on the truck."

Archie raised his hands over his head. "Okay, okay, I know when I'm whipped." He reached into the pocket of his thick baggy sweatpants and pulled out the money. He reached out, pressed it into my hand, then held me in a strong two-handed shake. "You're a fine man, George," he said. "Thank you for coming here."

Monty came up and tapped Archie on the shoulder. He had a stern look on his face. When Archie released my hand, I looked at the money—two twenties and a ten.

"I want you to tell me something, Uncle Archie." Monty was breathless about it. "I want to know, how good a boxer was my dad? Was he good? I mean, I know he was good, but was he, you know, the best you ever knew?"

In a blink, Archie's face changed to look like somebody who had just that minute rolled out of bed. He fisted his nose again. He turned around and looked at me. He got up, first rolling onto all fours, then pushing himself off the floor. He walked up to Monty and held his shoulders.

"Monty, in almost every way, your dad was a champion. Never has a stronger man walked into my gym. Strong in every way. Nobody ever saw Tommy fight that didn't love him. But things happen. A lot of things nobody can control. So in the end, I guess what they would say was that he was a good pug. He was always more than an 'opponent,' but not quite a contender."

Monty took it quietly, but I knew it wasn't

good enough for him. He headed for the door. Archie caught up to him. "And this much is a sure fact. I want you both to know this. Nobody, but nobody ever *wanted* to fight your father." Monty smiled up at him. He was into shaping himself a kind of superdad where there was none. And he could, since he didn't know anything about scrambled brains. Archie knew enough to give him something he could use. "A feared bonebreaker, he was," Archie said.

"Did he take the body?" I yelled from across the room.

"He was a *devil* at the body."

"I knew it," I said.

When we were back on the street, Archie stood leaning in his doorway. He asked Monty to go close the back of the truck.

"I know how your mother feels about it, George, but your father was a fighter, no matter what. He was a fighter first; then I signed on to train him. I figured if he was gonna do it, there weren't nobody who was gonna look after him better than his own brother. That was always my job." He paused, looked at his feet, shuffled them a little. "But, you know, after the Big Man fell, your ma . . . well I guess we was all left hurtin', wasn't we, George?"

I managed to nod, but it didn't matter because he wasn't looking at me.

"Now that we're practically neighbors, let us know when you have any more work, Archie," Monty said as he bounded back toward us. He never got the "forbidden" talk from Ma because, I suppose, she never thought it was necessary, figured it would trickle down through me. But he kind of knew how she felt, and he was being cute about it.

"Well, there is always stuff to be done." Archie looked right at me. "But I understand how it is. Though if you could ever get the chance to come by an' say hi. Just to say hi. . . ."

I pulled Monty by the arm and we left Archie waving in the doorway.

"Absolutely," Monty called.

"We'll see, Arch," I called.

All afternoon, Monty was itching to pick a fight with me. I wasn't into it. Finally he went out and left me alone. When Ma came home from work, he was still out.

"Is Coke still okay?" I smiled as I pulled two cans out of the refrigerator.

"Just barely," she said. I opened them both, gave her one. As she put on the water for spaghetti and pulled out a frying pan, I hopped up on the counter beside the stove.

"Ma, can you tell me how Dad died?"

She had the bottle of oil poised to pour. She stopped. "George? You know the answer to that. It was a cerebral hemorrhage."

"Ya, I know, but how did it happen?"

Her face turned red, and she got an angry look. Then, just as quickly, it washed away. She spoke evenly, quietly.

"Basically, Georgie, your dad was punched to death. By many men, over many years." Ma lit the burner, poured the oil, and stared into it. "Is that what you wanted to know?" she whispered.

"It answers my question. But no, it isn't what I *wanted* to know."

Monty came bouncing in the back door. Ma wiped a dish towel over her face before she turned around to kiss him. As soon as she did, her face froze. For the first time *ever*, I saw my mother look scared.

"Monty, you smell . . . peculiar," she said as he headed for the bathroom.

"I'll take a bath," he said, then shut the door behind him. From inside, he called back, "Ma, could you make me a steak tonight? A big one."

7
Legacy

The kind of crowd that was buzzing on the sidewalk ahead of me could only mean a fight. I always stop at a fight. It's spooky, I never enjoy them, they always make me kind of edgy, but I am powerless to look away.

This particular fight made me more uncomfortable than most, because when I shouldered my way to the front of the crowd, I found that one of the scufflers was my brother. The one who wasn't winning. Monty was lying flat on his back on the sidewalk, his head resting on the curb. His book bag had been flung into the street and there was a kid sitting on his chest. I could only see the back of the kid as he stared down into Monty's face, but he did have a ferret sitting on his head, also staring down at Monty.

I hung back for a minute, hoping Monty could work his way out of it alone, praying that he could. My fists were opening and closing at my sides. Buchanan wasn't saying anything, just sitting there. Monty, though, Monty was talking.

"Loser," he screamed from his very vulnerable position.

"You ain't getting up, you know," Buchanan said easily.

"I know I ain't, because you're a loser."

"I'm goin' easy on you Monty-boy, because I want all these people"—he made a sweeping gesture at the circle of kids looking on—"to know that I'm a lot nicer than folks say." He was having a fine time being in command.

"Ya, well what they know," Monty said, "is that you're sitting on me so long because you're a lonely loser, and because you like the way I feel."

Several boys laughed exaggerated laughs. Everyone enjoyed it when the Cannon got stuck. I put both hands on top of my head. I couldn't believe what my brother was doing, from where he was doing it.

The laughter got to Buchanan quickly. "That's enough, boy."

"Then let me up so I can kick your butt."

"Shut up," the Cannon yelled.

Monty started playing to the crowd, not even looking at Buchanan. "Hey," he said, "you can't just sit there forever. Either hit me or kiss me."

I knew immediately that he'd done it there. The kids went into whoops of laughter, Monty included. Before Buchanan moved, I broke toward him, but I couldn't get there in time. He pulled back and whipped Monty with a wicked, loud, open-hand slap in the mouth. The crowd went dead at the frightening crack. I jumped in, first punching the snarling ferret so hard that it sailed into the side of a parked car and crumpled into the gutter. Buchanan jumped to his feet and spun to meet me. Before he'd even planted his feet his quick, left hand was coming my way.

But he never had a chance. I drilled him with a straight, stiff right that knocked him three steps back. Without thinking I followed him, throwing violent punches with both hands, one for every step he took. With no ropes to catch him, the Cannon just reeled backward as I punched him in the mouth, in the mouth, in the mouth, senseless across the sidewalk. Finally, as the crowd gladly parted to let him through, Buchanan tumbled backward onto his rear, then jack-knifed, his skull ricocheting off the cement.

I didn't even care that Buchanan wasn't moving. I was floating. My heart was drumming, I couldn't feel my feet on the ground, and I held my fists still at chin level. I thought I might be sick. I turned to Monty and couldn't believe how far away he was. I had punched Buchanan all the way down thirty feet of sidewalk. As I walked back, Monty sat up, in the spot where he had been lying. A couple of kids were slapping him on the back and saying things into his ear, but he didn't acknowledge them. He was smiling slightly at me.

As I reentered the crowd, I too got many slaps on the back, and war whoops from the dreaded Cannon's many victims. At first I didn't pay any attention, but I couldn't avoid it. I was torn. My head and stomach were both spinning. I felt like I'd dropped a house on a witch. I felt like I'd saved a nation. I felt like I'd committed a crime.

My heart finally slowed a little. I reached my hand out to my brother. "We're outta here," I said.

He smiled again, took my hand, and got to his feet. When Monty went to pick up his books, a little guy in a tam-o'-shanter beat him to it. When he stood to hand Monty his books, I saw it was the Head. I looked back to check on Buchanan. He was gone. I looked in the gutter. Festus was gone too.

"What's with him?" I said when we were finally out of earshot of our fans. Monty was hanging a little behind me as we walked, and the Head was a little behind him. He looked like something out of

The Little Rascals with his head poking up through that ridiculous hat.

"He's my sidekick," Monty said loudly. "Dude's got to have a sidekick." Then he whispered in my ear, "Ever since I mouthed off to his old man, he kind of loves me."

I pulled away from him. "So you want to tell me what was going on back there?"

"I was getting my butt whipped, that's what," he said.

"Why, Monty?"

"Because he wrestled me, the big wus. If he would've boxed with me—"

The Head nodded righteously, silently.

"That's not the 'why' I'm asking about," I said.

"You mean why was I fighting at all? Hell, George, he was just . . . there. I was walking home with a few of my friends, and the guy started hassling me. I couldn't just let it happen. You wouldn't've. I'm not afraid of him, you know. I'm not."

"He's not afraid, George," the Head assured me.

I couldn't really argue with what Monty was saying, because I know he picked up that stuff from me. The problem was that for every rock he got from me, there were three more that he missed. "Lemme buy you a drink," I said, and pulled him into the Eastgate Pharmacy. But his adoring fandom was getting in the way of his thinking, so I asked the Head to stay outside.

"It's cool, Fred," Monty said. He took him by the shoulders and basically placed him on top of a fire hydrant, where he sat. "This won't take long."

We parked on a couple of red spinning stools at the fountain. It was the kind of fountain that looked right out of World War II or something. Not like Brigham's, where they try to make it old style, but old style because it was old, with a bell over the door that rang when you opened it. The place was all ours, because public school kids are banned from two until four because they're too rowdy. Not like Monty and me, with our ties on. The waitress with the ton of makeup and the pock-marked nose took our order, two mocha frappes.

"Maybe I don't want mocha," Monty said.

The waitress waited. "He didn't say anything," I told her, and she left. "Listen, Monty," I said. "I know how you feel, not wanting to be pushed around. And I think you have balls. But maybe taking it out on the street isn't the best idea."

"What, George, you want me to bring the guy home?"

"That mouth on you sure is getting to be a problem. You know what I'm saying. I'm saying I don't think you should be fighting. It's not in your best interest, I think."

The waitress came back and put two tall vase-shaped glasses in front of us, then filled them from an aluminum pitcher. I stood my spoon straight up in the frappe. Monty picked up his glass and pressed it against his lip, which was puffing slightly.

"C'mon, George," he mumbled against the glass. "You don't believe that. You *know* I had to stand with the Cannon. It's time I learned to take care of myself. Not that I don't appreciate it, but I can't let you do everything for me anymore." He liked to play simpleton, but Monty was no dope. He knew he was hammering me with my own rocks.

"Well . . ." I scrambled. "You *weren't* taking care of yourself."

"Think I didn't notice that, George? But I'll get better. I'm learning all the time. And when I saw you, what you did to stupidass Buchanan . . . I had goose bumps. It was beautiful."

"It was *not* beautiful," I growled. "It made me sick."

He put his glass down on the yellow Formica, dipped his finger into the frappe, and licked it off. "You're lyyy-ingg," he sang.

I was getting tempted to whack him myself. The waitress came and asked if we wanted more. I didn't answer. Monty shook his head at her as I took a long swallow.

"You don't know *any*thing," I said, wiping away

my mustache. "I mean, before, I thought you didn't know anything, but now I think you know even less. About fighting, about *not* fighting. And what you don't know is gonna get you killed if you don't smarten up."

"Oh, and you know *everything*, is that right?"

I knew that I didn't know everything, and every day I became more aware of that. Monty spotted that weakness and jabbed at it.

"I really don't need you telling me what to do all the time. I've learned a lot already. I'm not gonna get hurt. I've learned all your moves. And I remember everything Dad ever taught me."

"What? What Dad taught you?"

"Ya, that's right. I remember it all. And Dad was the best."

"Monty." I tried to calm down, even though he'd gotten my heart pounding again. "You were just a shrimp. You don't remember anything—"

"Shut up, George. Dad taught me it all. And I remember it. Everything that made him a great fighter is right up here." He tapped himself on the temple.

It sure is all in your head, I thought. Because with a lifetime record of forty-nine wins and forty-three losses, my dad was not a great fighter. Even I knew that.

"I don't think he taught you to lie on your back and trash-talk the guy who's sitting on you," I said as nicely as I could. Monty was making me feel bad, afraid to say too much. But I had to point out what was wrong with this picture.

He got off his stool. Leaning into me, he tapped his head again. "Rule number seven: Learn from your mistakes, don't repeat them."

"Good," I said. "So you'll quit fighting."

"You're not my father, you know, George," he said.

"No, I'm not. And *you're* not gonna be, either." I knew he wasn't listening to what I had to say, and I didn't know how to fix it. Maybe I should have let the Cannon drop me, to show Monty better. Maybe I should have knocked sense into Monty instead. He was right—there were still a lot of holes in what I knew. Where the hell did you go, Dad? I could sure use a hand. You're the only one who knew all this.

Monty slid his barely touched drink in front of me, then marched out of the drugstore.

"And I *don't like mocha*," he said. The bell rang as he strutted out to the sidewalk to collect his sidekick.

8

The Devil's Workshop

Our mother didn't feel that hanging out with Nat the superintendent was a great thing, and as far as we could tell neither did anyone else in the building. They all called him Baby Nat, because he had only the one tooth, and because he was all round and soft and fluffy white, a lot like a baby would be if you blew it up to full size.

"Don't you think it's awesome the way Nat gets to go around picking at his seat and wearing the same clothes every day?" Monty said as we went down to the basement. Nat was going to show us how to clean the furnace. "It's like, how did this guy ever get to be in the adult world acting like he does?"

"He's not in the adult world," I said. "Haven't you seen the way everyone around here treats the guy? They treat him like a kid. They treat him worse than a kid, even. They treat him like something they'd have to walk around if they saw him in the street."

Nat was mopping the carpet in the hall outside the basement apartments when we showed up.

"I didn't know you were supposed to mop rugs," I said.

"Shampooing," he said. "Gotta do it every oncet in a while." He pushed the mop along slowly, spraying foam on the floor ahead of him and then mopping it right up again. "Ain't you never noticed how nice 'n' shiny all the rugs is in this buildin'?"

"I guess I did," I said, "but I didn't think anybody worked at it."

"See, there it go again," he said. "Ain't no 'preciation for what-all I do 'round here. None."

"I knew it, Nat." Monty jumped in. "I knowed it all straight up. And I done telled all uh ma friends down to the school. I tells 'em all the time that we's gut the shiniest old rugs back to our place, and that it's ol' Baby Nat that is responsible."

Nat laughed his loudest rooster laugh, the Carolina crow. "I swear, you a good ol' boy, there, Montgomery. A rascal, you is." Nat dropped his mop in the middle of the hallway and grabbed

Monty in a playful headlock. "Boys, lets go clean us a furnace."

It was eight o'clock Saturday morning when we went into the furnace room. Ma had gone to work already, so we were able to go down. We didn't exactly sneak around to spend time with Nat, but we couldn't really make it obvious either, since Ma saw hanging out with Nat as barely better than hanging with Archie.

"Gotta stop in the office to get my equipment," Nat said. We followed him to the room that was his office as well as his apartment and broom closet. Written in Day-Glo green marker on the door was "The Nat Hole." It was twelve feet long by nine feet wide, and pipes of all kinds ran through it in every direction, making it seem even smaller. The air was thick from steam and Nat's own smells.

"You sleep on that little cot?" Monty asked.

"I do."

"Cool," Monty said.

"Cool it ain't, young man. But it ain't the street, neither."

I found myself poking around the walls of the room.

"Don't get y'self sick now." Nat startled me as I stared up close at his three calendars of naked women: 1972, 1976, and 1984.

"I wasn't going to touch them," I said.

He laughed. "Go on ahead if you want to. I wasn't talking about them, anyhow. I meant this." He slapped a white, padded pipe above my head and inhaled deeply in the dust that rained down. "Asbestos." He laughed.

Nat gathered his equipment, which turned out to be a pile of rags, a bucket, and a whisk broom. Before we left he took a deep drink from a tall, clear bottle that was lying on the cot.

The big old furnace was breathing heavy. It was hard to believe all the effort we could see down in the basement was what caused the weak puffs of warm air that came up through the floor of the apartment once in a while. It was mummified in the same dusty padding that was on the pipes in Nat's room. The fat tin pipes that carried the heat upstairs were attached to the ceiling by coat hangers and fishing line, and were patched with tape at nearly every seam.

"So you're in charge of everything down here, huh, Nat?" Monty said.

"Yep. It's a lot of work, 'specially with an old place like this. But I keep it all together, with a little spit, a little chewing gum, and with this here." He tapped a finger on the side of his head. "And I do it just for you-all. I hope you remember that. A guy just wants to be 'preciated, y'know." Nat pulled a screen out from the back of the furnace. He slapped it, raising a black cloud of soot.

"I 'preciate you, Nat," Monty said.

"Sure, Nat," I said. "I think all the tenants *a-preciate*"—I looked at Monty—"the work you do."

"No they don't," Monty said.

"Shut up, Monty," I said. "You don't know what you're talking about."

"Sure he do, George. It's okay, let him speak it."

"Mr. O'Neill, the guy across the hall from us, calls you 'The Pervert in the Cellar.'"

"What's that you pulled out of the furnace there?" I jumped in before Monty could say more. "Monty wants to see it too." I grabbed Monty by the back of the shirt and pushed him toward the furnace.

Nat did his cackling laugh again. "Relax, Mr. George. I don't mind what people say. Long's ever'body don't feel that way. They don't, do they?"

"Ya, pretty much," Monty said.

Nat laughed again, but not nearly as hard as before. I showed Monty the furnace up close, squeezing the back of his neck and growling in his ear like Ma does, to say "That's enough talking for now, thank you." The other names we'd heard used for Nat in the year he'd been around started running through my head. "Sludge," "The Bowels of the Building," "The Creature from the Black Lagoon" (the Goon, for short). Old man Cruz on the second floor called him "El Puerco."

"Yo, Nat, those people callin' you the names, you want me to kick some butt for ya?"

"What *is* your problem?" I yelled. "You talk like a goon lately."

"I'm not a goon," Monty said. "I'm just tough."

"You're too stupid to know the difference," I snapped. I had to back off. This speech was building, but I had to remind myself: You're gonna make it worse. You're gonna make it worse. . . .

"Thank you, but no thank you, Mr. Monty," Nat said. Monty's offer seemed to be the thing that finally made Nat a little sad.

We didn't even realize that we'd gotten dirty, but when we got out under the white light of the hallway, I saw that Monty was covered in a sort of chalk-dust gray powder, and so was I. Nat had the same thing, but his was shinier, mixed with oily sweat.

"How's about some lunch, boys?" Nat said. It was only ten thirty in the morning.

"Excellent," Monty said.

"No, thanks, Nat. We should go," I said.

"Come on, now. Where you-all got to get to this time?"

"Ya," Monty said. "Where we-all got to get to?"

The only responses that were coming to mind were "Well, you smell, Nat. And our mother doesn't want us hanging around with you. And I'm afraid of what your food might be like. . . ." He was so friendly to us, I couldn't say anything but "Sure, Nat. Lunch would be nice, I guess."

We sat on shaky wooden chairs, using a third grader's desk for a table. Nat turned on the TV to wrestling, then pulled a deli package out of the short, brown, square refrigerator sitting in the corner. He grabbed his bottle off the cot, then sat at the desk with us.

"Have a swallow, boys?" he said, unscrewing the top, then aiming the bottle at me. It had a thick mint smell, but also a thick Nat smell. The thought of the liquid inside made me gag.

"No, thank you," I said with my lips held tight. He pointed the bottle at Monty. "He doesn't want any either," I said, staring at Monty.

"Maybe after we eat, then," Nat said. He took a long drink. "You-all don't know what you're missin' though. Crème de menthe, this is. Some fine stuff. A tenant in this here building give it to me, too. Mr. English. Only Christmas present I ever got on the job, though it probly don't hardly count anyway since Mr. English only give it to me one night when we sat on the stoop together after he was at some party and his old lady wouldn't let him in the apartment. Do it count, you think, if a present already got three fingers drunk out of it by the time you get it?"

Mr. English was the guy who called Nat "Sludge."

"I don't see why not," I lied.

"Well I don't either, then. I'll say I got a present even though I ain't heard boogety-shoo from the man since that night." He took another big swig, then unwrapped the package. There were two knockwursts inside.

"Damn," Nat said, holding up one knockwurst in each filthy hand. "I thought for certain there was at least three of these porkies left."

"Hey, don't worry about it," I said. "I never eat before noon. Really."

"I eat before noon all the time," Monty said, then pointed to one of Nat's hands. "But I'm not eating *that*."

Nat looked at his hands like he couldn't figure out what was wrong. "I got some chips, then. You boys gotta like chips. And some sardines." Nat pulled a bag of chips from a box under the desk, and a can of sardines out of the top drawer. Monty pulled back when he saw, and smelled, that both were already opened. That was enough for me, too.

"No kidding, Nat, we have to be going," I said, tugging my brother by the sleeve. "But thanks, we had a good time."

"A good ol' time," Monty chirped.

"You's a certain pistol, kid. I tell you what. Say now boys, I got nothin' tomorrow, because it's Sunday and ain't no reason in the world for a hard-workin' man to go killin' hisself no fu'ther on the seventh day. But later on, on Monday afternoon, I got a fine job. That's when I got to go out on the roof an' clean the gutters. You-all want to see how it's done, be here late afternoon, after I get back from the dump."

It sounded like a good time, but one we could catch some hell for if anyone saw us. "Sounds good," I said. "We'll see."

"Damn straight," Monty said. "We're there."

We got upstairs and cleaned up before Ma came home. The tub was grimy and the bathroom had an odor that we had picked up off Nat's room, but a little scrubbing and some lavender air freshener took care of it.

———

At the breakfast table on Monday morning, Ma asked me if I was busy that afternoon.

"Not really, Ma. Why, what's up?"

"They're having one of those tenants' meetings, and I can't get out of work in time. The building's activists—the ones with nothing to do—always schedule these things early so the rest of us don't horn in on their dominion. It's at five o'clock. George, do you think you could go to it for me? I have no idea what it's about—probably routine stuff."

Since Saturday, I had gotten more excited about going up on the roof with Nat. But I had also gotten more nervous about it, so I was actually not too upset that I had a reason not to go now. "Sure, Ma. I'll take care of it. I'll give you a report when you get home." Monty stared at me across the table, like "what are you doing?"

"Thanks George. That's a big help. I'm really swamped at work right now, but I don't like to miss these things. I like to stay involved. If there's any kind of decision to be made, go ahead and vote in my place. I trust your judgment." She sipped her coffee quickly. I nodded and winked at her. "I'm sorry guys, but I have to be running now." She grabbed her briefcase and kissed us both on the head. "I promise this is only temporary.

Next week will be different."

"Don't you worry a lick now, ma'am," Monty said to her as she ran out to make her train.

"I'll take care of things," I said.

Monty turned to me. "What's wrong with you? Did you forget we're going up on the roof this afternoon? You don't want to go to that boring meeting, do you?"

"Maybe I do. Anyway, I said I'd go so I'm going."

Monty stood up while he finished his juice. He grabbed his books and a pancake and headed out. "Too bad," he said. "You're going to miss a lot of fun."

"So are you. You aren't going up there without me, pal."

He spun around in the doorway. "What? Why not?"

"Listen, it would've been risky enough anyway, but I really think that you shouldn't be up there if I'm not around."

Monty put his hand on his hip after he finished the pancake. He looked bored with me. "I don't know what you're talking about, and neither do you. What I do know is I don't need you for *everything*, George."

"Well, you don't have to understand, just do it."

He balled up another pancake and jammed the whole thing in his mouth. Then he left without saying anything.

The meeting was held in the building's "function room," which was an unused studio apartment on the first floor, about five times the size of Nat's place. There was a long folding table at the front of the room with a plate of dry cookies, some hard bread, and a small cardboard house full of doughnut holes. There was nothing to drink, so nobody could choke down any of the stuff. Fifteen people were there besides me, the same people who always seemed to be making noise about something, except for Old John. Old John was a quiet guy who didn't seem to belong here. Even with all these folks, the room seemed like a wide-open waste of space. I wondered why they didn't just let Nat have it.

"Oh look, it's young George," Martha the bearded lady said. She came over and patted me on the head even though I was just as tall as she was. "Are you here representing your mother?" she said sweetly.

"Ya," I said, although the way she said it made me feel small and foolish.

"Good." She spun and yelled at the others. "Then there'll be no one else coming. Let's do it. I

93

say we get rid of the slob."

"This shouldn't take too much time," Mr. English said. "I say we dump him right now. Get his sludgy old butt out of our building." He grabbed his stomach and burped.

"What's the story here?" I asked.

"We're voting to get rid of that embarrassment we got in the cellar, Baby Nat," said Mrs. Fine, a fifty-year-old blond woman with a big round belly who was wearing spandex pants. Nat was always saying what a fox she was.

"Why? What did he do?" I said.

"He's a peeg," old man Cruz said.

"So are you and you and you and you," I said in my head as I looked around the room. But I held my tongue.

"He's just not right," Martha said. "I haven't slept a wink since he moved into the building. Not one wink."

It shows is what I thought. But what I said was, "But has he done anything to you?"

"Well, no," she said. "But what am I supposed to do, sit around waiting for him to molest me?"

"Don't hold your breath." That one slipped out, but I mumbled.

"What?" she said. "What was that?" Old John ate a doughnut hole. The first one eaten.

"I said, ma'am, that Nat's harmless. He's not going to do anything to you. He's a nice man."

"No, he's a peeg" was all Cruz seemed to want to say. "Weirdo, loser, mental case, bad seed, creepy," they all seemed to say as a mob. I was reconsidering turning Monty loose to beat them all up.

"Let's vote," Mrs. Fine said as she pulled a lipstick-drenched cigarette out of her mouth.

"Dump him. Dump him. Dump him. Dump him," they all said. "Kill him," somebody said from the back of the crowd. It seemed that everyone voted to get rid of Nat except Old John, who was pawing at the food.

"John?" I said. "How about you? Do you feel the same way about it?"

John turned slowly around, picking crumbs out of his thick gray mustache. "No. No, son, I don't feel the same way they do. I never feel the same way they do. I don't see anything wrong with that Nat feller. But you see, they always outvote me."

"That's right, we do," Mr. English said. "I'll call the landlord in the morning and tell him what we decided. Right now, it's *Wheel of Fortune* and high-balls in my apartment."

"No," I said as they all started out.

"No what?" Mr. English said, as if he wanted to hit me.

"No, you can't just throw Nat out like that. You have to give him a chance."

"Oh yes, we can," he said. "The landlord don't want no trouble from us. He does whatever we say. And we say Sludge goes."

"No," I said more firmly.

"What makes you think you can say no, little boy?" Martha was getting particularly irritated with me.

"I'm voting in place of my mother," I said. I knew I was pulling out the big gun when I mentioned Ma. She carried a lot of weight around here. Working at the State Rehab, she had worked with half the people in the building or their families at one time or another. One right word from her at the office could sometimes make life a whole lot easier for somebody. "And Ma happens to like Nat very much." She had never actually come out and said what she thought of Nat, but I knew that she would agree that what was going on here was unfair. And it felt good to hear them all suck wind at once.

They were confused. They muttered to each other. English made a stand. "So? Your mother doesn't make all the rules around here, you know."

I didn't respond. They muttered some more. Old John laughed out loud.

"So what are you saying?" Mrs. Fine said.

"I'm saying that Nat does good work, and that he never does any of you any harm. Cut him some slack. Give him one more month. If you still want to get rid of him, then have another meeting."

They all looked at one another, shrugging. Mr. English looked back at me and nodded, but he wasn't happy about it. They filed out, leaving me alone with the old food and Old John. John gathered up the boxes of food.

"They always do this, the fools," he said. "Nothing to drink, nobody eats. I take 'em home. They go down fine with milk. Want some?" He laughed.

"No," I said.

He shuffled out. "Nice move," Old John said, pointing a long finger at me from the doorway. "It felt good to finally win one."

Walking up the stairs, I had a feeling of power in me. I made a bunch of adults do what I said, even though it was really my mother's weight I was throwing around. But most of all, I felt like I had done something that was truly right. I couldn't wait to tell Monty how I'd rescued our man Nat.

But the apartment was empty when I got there. It was six o'clock, and I already knew Ma was working late, but Monty should have been there. I sat in front of the TV to wait for somebody to come home and hear my story. But then I remembered.

I ran up the back stairwell, with the metal railing and concrete walls. When I got to the top, I pushed open the trapdoor to the roof. I looked around in all directions with just my head and arms outside. They weren't there. I walked down five flights to The Nat Hole.

When I got there I heard Nat talking inside. I listened by the door while he finished one of his great, slow stories.

" . . . So I says to him, I says, 'Mr. Judge, your honor, suh. I don't know rightly why I done broke into that there store. It was the middle of the night an', well, I guess I had my head tore off some, and well this little bird just sorta flew up an' landed on my shoulder an' he said, "Nat, you just *got* to get your body into that store and get yourself some cigarettes right this very minute."' So you know what he says. He was a good ol' boy, that judge. He says to me, 'Nat, that's quite a coincidence, because that same little bird come up to me this mornin' and said, "Judge, you just *got* to give ol' Nat ninety days on the prison farm."' An' he slams down that gavel an' next thing I knowed, I's pickin' peas." Nat laughed his rooster laugh at his own story. Then I heard Monty laugh too, but it was a fuzzy, weak laugh. I knocked hard and Nat said to come on in.

Nat was sitting behind the desk like a teacher, with Monty on the other side. The room was full of sharp cigar stench, in addition to the usual smell. Monty's skin was greenish, and his eyes were watery as he stared stupidly at the blank TV. He didn't seem to notice me.

"Join the party, Georgie," Nat said. I ignored him, walking right up to my brother. I grabbed his chin and made him look at me. He stunk, like mint and tobacco. He stunk like Nat. I whipped my head around to look at Nat, who was smiling, surrounded by stacks of naked women magazines. My hands and legs were shaking. I could barely make words come out of my mouth.

"What the hell is the matter with you, Nat?" I said while lifting Monty off the chair.

"Take me upstairs, huh, George?" Monty said. I threw his arm over my shoulder and walked him out.

Nat got up and followed us to the door. It seemed he was only now figuring out that something might be wrong with all this. "I'm sorry, George. I'm sorry. I didn't mean no harm. I didn't mean to do Monty no harm. Are you gonna have to rat me out now, George? Do you have to?"

He stood in his doorway while we walked away.

"George, I'm sick," Monty said when we got inside our apartment. Ma still wasn't home yet. I propped him in front of the toilet, and he got sick for five minutes, then lay on the floor with his face against the cool porcelain.

"No time for that, man," I said, and hustled him into bed in his underwear. While he slept, I went back and cleaned the bathroom. Suddenly, there he was, curled around the base of the toilet again. I heard Ma coming up the stairs and just managed to get him back to the bed before she got there. He was out for good immediately.

"Hi, Ma," I said. "Long day, huh?"

She sighed. "Endless." She sat in the kitchen, pulled off a shoe, and rubbed her foot. "Where's Monty?" she said.

"He's in bed already."

"At seven o'clock?"

"He wasn't feeling too well, he said."

She leaned forward in the chair as if she were going to get up and go in. "Is he sick?"

I put my hands out to reassure her, to keep her in her seat. "He's fine, Ma. He's just overtired, I think. Don't worry, I watched him."

She fell back in the chair. "Whew, thanks George. I'm glad you're here. I think I'll be going right to bed myself, now that I think of it."

"Good idea, Ma."

"By the way, how did the tenants' meeting go?"

I was also starting to feel tired. "It was fine. But could I tell you about it in the morning? I'd like to get to bed too. I ain't feelin' all too good my own self."

She raised one eyebrow at me. "Come again?"

"I'm beat, Ma." I kissed her on the cheek and backed away. "I'll talk to you in the morning."

Monty was snoring when I got undressed. He would lie completely still, then roll and thrash all around in the bed for a few seconds. Then he'd be still again. I thought about Nat. Baby Nat, stupid Nat. I thought about what I was going to have to do. He didn't mean any harm. He didn't even know he'd done anything. Well then, that makes it even worse, right? Monty hadn't moved for a while, so I checked on him. He still smelled, but he wasn't really all that bad. And no matter what, this does not make *them* right. But they'll have a good time with it anyway. What happens to a guy like Nat when he loses a place like this?

Something caught in my throat; my head

started hurting at the temples. I had no idea why I was feeling like this, but I went to the mirror to stare it down. I looked at my face in the mirror and noticed my jaw muscles flexing away. I stared at myself until the feeling went away, reminding myself what a son of a bitch Nat was, how I fought for him, how he screwed us up.

"Besides," I said to my reflection, "Nat isn't my responsibility, Monty is. Nat's on his own." I went to bed.

By the time Ma came out of her room at six thirty the next morning, I was dressed, waiting for her at the table. I ratted Nat out. I told her about his drinking on the job, about his prison stories that only Monty and me knew about, and about his offering me booze and cigars. I didn't say anything about Monty. I'd handle Monty myself. That is, if I could anymore.

9

Slipping Grip

Ma had to fly off to work again very early, before Monty could haul himself out of bed. She apologized again, but I wished she wouldn't. She was doing what she had to. That's what we do.

"But I have an idea about how we might make things a little better for you and Monty," she said. "I've been thinking about it for a while, but now, with this Nat thing and all, I'm sure it's a good idea. We'll talk about it tonight when I get home."

"Fine," I said, holding up her coat by the shoulders for her to slip into. Every once in a while Ma came up with a project or a hobby for Monty and me, to keep us stimulated. Like when we built that giant bird feeder that the squirrels live in now. We'd go at it for a week or so and that would be that. I figured it was one of those.

After she left, I mixed a chocolate milk. I flattened my hand over the top of the glass and shook it like crazy so that it got good and frothy, then licked my palm. I make great chocolate milk.

When I walked into the bedroom, Monty was talking, gasping really, like he had sand in his throat. "Water. George, Ma, somebody, could I please have a glass of water?" His eyes weren't even open.

"Here," I said, lifting him up by the head into sitting position. "This is what you need." I stood beside the bed and watched while he drained the glass of chocolate milk and kept trying to drink, sucking at the bubbles, after there was really nothing left.

"Please," he said, holding out the glass, "may I have some more?"

"Not feeling too good, huh?"

He fell back on the bed and pulled the sheet over his head. "No."

"Well, you can have more, but there's not going to be any more room service. Get up and get dressed and I'll have breakfast for you in the kitchen."

"Geoooorrge," he whined, still under the sheet. "I can't go to school today, I'm sick."

"Oh ya, right. 'Uh, Sister, my brother Monty won't be in to sixth grade today. He got polluted last night—you know how it is, don't ya, babe?'"

"Well, George, you don't have to tell her *that*."

"I don't have to tell her anything, 'cause you're going to be there. Just give the chocolate milk a couple of minutes to work and then come out. Trust me, chocolate milk fixes anything."

I was flipping the last of the French toast from the pan to the plate when Monty crept into the kitchen. "Well there you go," I said. "How you doin'?"

He stood in the doorway tucking in his shirt in slow motion, like it was a lot of work. "I feel all right, I think. The chocolate milks might work if I keep drinking them. It feels like the first one is starting to wear off already, though." I handed him another, already mixed. He wrapped both hands around the glass, like a baby with a bottle. "How do you know so much about fixing a guy up like this, George?"

I plopped the plate in the middle of the table. "This ain't the first time I had to play early morning cornerman to some big stupid pug. Eat," I said.

Eat he did. For the first ten minutes of breakfast we didn't say another word. Monty tore at that pile of French toast just like a dog at the garbage. I had one piece, he had five. Every piece he washed down with loud gulps of chocolate milk. I sipped coffee. Each time he finished one piece of toast, he would look up, still chewing the last one, and point at the stack with his knife. "Go ahead, you take it," I said, and I just kept smiling at him. When it was all gone, he sat back satisfied in his chair. "Whew," he said. A tight, round belly stuck out from his wiry body. I finished my coffee.

"Feeling all right now, are ya?" I said, leaning over and patting him on the shoulder.

"Oh, man, George, this was great. You saved my life. I think I'm gonna make it."

"Well I'm glad," I said. I went to the corner, where we kept the duffel bags we used to carry our books. I picked both of them up. They were loaded, probably twenty book pounds apiece. I dropped them both with a big thunk at Monty's feet. "Carry my books," I said with a big smile.

"Oh, Georgie, no. You can't, please?"

"Okay," I said. "I could carry both book bags and you could carry me on your back, if that would be easier."

"Aahhhh," Monty yelled, pulling his own hair with both hands. I waited for it to pass. He picked up the bags and we went out.

On the way out the front door, I put my arm around his shoulders. "Now that you're feeling better," I said, "let's have a talk, you and me."

"I knew it," he said. "I just knew it. Please,

George, I can't handle a 'cracks of society' story this morning." I was in the habit of telling about people who slip through the cracks. He was at the point where he'd rather slip than listen to one more. He walked down the stairs ahead of me. I watched from behind as his knobby knees kept banging into each other as he hauled the bags.

"I figure you know what I want to talk about, right?" I said as we hit the sidewalk.

"Ya," he said. "Nat's in trouble, isn't he?" He didn't look at me when he said it, trying to be cool despite the sweat that was forming on his lip.

"Smooth, Monty. Ya, you're right, Nat is in trouble. But, ah, can you think of anyone else who might be in some deep sneakers? Like, maybe, somebody who's here with us now?"

"I don't suppose it's you?"

"No it's not me," I barked at him. "What the hell is wrong with you? Cigars and booze with Nat? Are you just stupid, Monty, or what? Did you eat the old sardines out of the desk while you were at it? You know, you really should have gotten loaded first, *then* gone up on the roof to clean gutters. That would have been a rush, wouldn't it?" Once I started yelling at Monty, I couldn't stop. He kept on walking, hunched under the book bags, looking at the ground, while I circled him, walking backward, bending low and looking up into his eyes. I couldn't stop flapping my arms at him while I yelled.

People on the street were starting to stare. Like I was the bad guy. Monty was starting to look a little weak. I grabbed both bags from him and threw them over my shoulders. "What do you have to say for yourself?" I said.

He was still walking hunched, without the bags. "George, if I don't get another chocolate milk soon, I'm gonna heave." But before he could do anything, he spotted, a half block ahead and coming our way, Buchanan. And Festus. As if somebody had thrown a switch, Monty the hunchback became Monty the stud. Walking tall, swaggering. His left hand curled into a fist and swung like a wrecking ball at his side. As soon as they locked eyes, Buchanan crossed to the other side of the street.

"How did you do that?" I said.

"I'm developing an aura," he said. He checked over his shoulder to see that the Cannon was out of sight before doubling over again and moaning, "Chocolate milk?"

I sat him on the curb with the book bags on either side of him and I went into the superette. I came out with a quart of the ready-mixed stuff.

"Here," I said. "I can't make you any promises, 'cause I don't know if the store-bought kind works." Monty threw his head back and chugged like he'd been in the desert for a year. Then he burped.

"Is that all you have to say?" I said, sticking out my hand and pulling him up. He just shrugged.

"Fine, then, Monty. I'm afraid I'm going to have to ground you."

"What?" he yelled at me. "You can't ground me. George, you're crazy."

"I assume this is still the liquor talking, Monty, so I'll let that pass. But I am serious."

Monty threw the half-full carton on the street. "No way. Uh-uh. You don't have grounding power."

I pointed to the ground. "You see that? Now, you want to be *grounded*?"

"Sure, George, you can *pound* me, in my condition, that is. But you cannot make me stay in the house."

"I could talk to Ma about it. And maybe about some of your other pastimes."

"Rat," he said. But that ended the argument pretty quickly. Monty stood there, frowning at me, but without anything else he could do. He did start turning a little green, though. He looked at the street, where the chocolate milk he'd thrown down in his fit was running out into the gutter.

"Not gonna make it, are you?" I said. He shook his head. "Go ahead," I told him. "Go on home."

"What are you gonna tell them at school?" he said.

"I'll come up with something." I waved a finger at him. "You see what you make me do?"

"Big shit," I think he muttered. Monty turned and headed back toward home. I watched him, thinking about the sentence I had just given him. Since it was a secret grounding, he had to stay in the house *and* keep Ma from finding out about it at the same time. All he had the strength left to do was drag the book bag on the sidewalk behind him.

"Stop that," I called. "You're gonna wear a hole in it before you get home." He didn't answer me. I figured the strain just got to be too much for him, because he stopped right there and sat down on the curb. I went back, helped him up, and carried the bag home for him.

"Now I'm gonna be late, so I have to make up stories for both of us. See what happens?" I knew he wasn't going to answer. When we got to the front steps, I gave him back the bag. He wobbled up the steps with it.

"And I am not a rat," I said. "I'm in charge, that's all."

He turned around in the doorway just as I backed away. "I happen to know that Joe Louis missed school *every* day at my age," he said, then slammed the door.

I walked into the bedroom when I got home from school. Monty was lying on his bed with his eyes closed. As I changed into my dungarees, he talked to me.

"George, what's gonna happen to Nat?"

"I figure they'll fire him and make him leave the building."

"I don't think it's fair."

"Monty, grow up." I yanked the black Bruins sweatshirt down over my head. "I liked Nat too, but he has to go and that's all there is to it. He's a dangerous guy to have around, not because he's mean, but because he doesn't know any better. And since we found out that you don't know how to act right either, we have to protect you from yourself. It's like we have to childproof the whole building because of you."

Monty sat down on the bed and shook his head. "Ya, y'know, George, I don't know what happened. That mint stuff Nat was drinking . . . he poured it into this tall glass with a lot of ice. I checked it out, and it didn't look like much, didn't taste like much, smelled kind of nice. . . ."

"And the cigars, Monty? Looked kind of nice? Smelled kind of nice, did they?"

"Hell no. George, I didn't smoke one of them stinky old things. Nat offered me one, but I didn't take it. I wound up getting sick just because I breathed near it."

The way Monty explained himself, everything so confusing to him, it was hard to keep being mad. But I tried. "I'm very disappointed in you, Monty. I really am. You're not stupid, man."

Monty got up and walked across to the closet. He went inside and closed the door behind him. This was his spot to think when he needed to be alone in our small apartment. Ma and I would have to pretend we didn't know he was in there. "I'm disappointed in me too," his muffled voice said.

The front door opened. At first I was surprised, but then I heard my mother's heels clacking down the hallway. Still, it was only three thirty, and lately she hadn't been coming home until at least seven.

"How long am I grounded for?" Monty's voice said just before Ma came into the room. "You never set a limit."

"Let me think about it. I'll get back to you. Hi, Ma. How come you're home so early? You didn't get laid off or anything, did you?"

"Nice to see you too, George. Relax. My job is secure. Where's your brother?"

I pointed at the closet door with my thumb. Ma walked close to the door.

"Hello, Monty," she said. "Honey, are you feeling better?"

Monty pushed the door open very slowly with his foot. The hinge creaked for about five seconds. Monty had a panicked look on his face, peeking up out of the pile of shoes and jackets.

"Are you feeling better today, sweetie?" Ma repeated when she saw him. "You do look a little pale."

From behind her, I kept nodding my head at Monty and mouthing "I'm fine. I'm fine," to tell him it was okay to answer.

"I'm fine," he said, and nodded like a marionette, but his eyes were shifting back and forth guiltylike.

"Come on up out of there," Ma said to him, pulling him by the hand. "I want to talk to you both." She was right, Monty was pale again, but when she put her arm around him and walked him over to the bed, he seemed to realize that she didn't know what had happened. He turned flesh colored again.

We all sat on the bed. "Guys," Ma said, "I haven't been such a great mother lately, and I'm sorry."

"Don't say that," I told her. "I mean it, I don't want you to say that anymore. We've got no problems with the way things run around here, right, Monty?"

"That's right, Ma," Monty squealed. He overdid it a bit, but I knew it was because he was just happy to be alive, not sick, and not in too much trouble. I gave him a look so that he'd tone it down.

"That's kind of you, boys, but I know how it really is. There's something missing from your lives, and I just can't fix it by myself. So, what I did was I contacted the Big Brothers and Big Sisters Association. We're going to get you guys a big brother."

Monty smiled. "Couldn't you call them back and get us a big sister instead?"

"Monty!" Ma tried to act shocked, but she laughed instead. Then she turned to look at me.

"Why?" I said.

"Because, George, the two of you spend too much time sort of skulking around by yourselves, and god knows what kind of characters you'll be meeting up with. You need some direction, some guidance. You need someone you can spend time with and share interests with."

I was only half listening by now, so I had to wait to be sure she was done. "What's wrong with *me?*" I said.

"There's nothing wrong with you, George. Nothing. It's just that, well, I don't think it would hurt to have a man's influence around here. The right kind of man's influence."

I got up and stood beside the bed. "Well we don't need him," I said. "You've just made a mistake, that's all. I think you are underestimating us. Between you and me I think we have things pretty well taken care of around here. So," I said as if there would be no more discussion, "why don't you just call them back and tell them thanks, but we won't be needing them to send us anybody."

"George," Ma said, breathing out heavily, "it had occurred to me that you wouldn't warm right up to this idea, but I want you to give it a chance. Please?"

"Ya, give the guy a chance, George," Monty said. "If we don't like him, we'll make hamburger out of him."

"I'd really rather you didn't, whether you like him or not," she said.

I nodded, then shook her hand lifelessly. The problem was that I was losing control of Monty, and she could sense it. I had to get it back, and the first step would be to get rid of this Big Brother fool.

"Okay, then," she said. "Now, I have to go and take care of our Nat problem. That's the real reason I'm early. I called the landlord and Mr. English, since he's head vigilante around here, and we're going down to have a talk with Nat."

"You mean he might be able to stay?" Monty said.

"I . . . wouldn't expect so, Monty. No."

"Oh," Monty said sadly.

"I'll only be a short while," Ma said as she got up to leave. "When I come back, we'll have a nice dinner, together for a change."

"I still feel bad about what they're gonna do to Nat," Monty said after Ma was gone. I couldn't think about Nat right now.

"*I'm* the big friggin' brother around here," I said. Monty then realized I didn't think the idea was as funny as he did.

"George, lighten up, man. This big brother thing might not be such a bad deal. Think about it—it's your chance to have a big brother, and it's my chance to have a *decent* big brother."

"I don't know why you think it's so funny," I said. "You're the reason this is happening. Ma thinks I'm failing with you, so she's bringing in the damn marines." I paced from the closet to the bed to the love seat and back again as I tried to figure things out. "This is *my* job," I said, poking myself hard in the chest. "This job was left to *me*, nobody else," I yelled.

"I did all this?" Monty said.

"I got no time for this, Monty." I took him by the arm. I led him back to the closet and opened the door. "Why don't you just go back in there and leave me alone for a while. I have to think." He went in and pulled the door closed behind him. I lay down on the bed and stared at the ceiling.

We stayed just like that for twenty minutes, until Ma's heels tapped down the hallway again. Monty called from behind the closet door just as she walked in.

"So, what happened?" he said, anxious.

"He's gone," Ma answered. "He was gone when we got there. Just cleared right out. The room looks like nothing but a broom closet. If it wasn't for the smell, you'd never know he'd been there."

"He didn't have a whole lot of stuff anyway," I said.

She snapped her head in my direction. "How do you know what he had?" I felt my ears get red.

"Oh, he was always saying that he didn't own anything that he couldn't just pack up and carry off on his back."

"Well." Ma looked at me suspiciously. "Well, I

guess he didn't. I had no idea the conditions he was living under. He must have lived like an animal down there, the poor thing. It's no wonder . . ."

"Ma." Monty's voice came out small. She walked toward it and he pushed the door open. He'd changed into his sweatsuit while he was in there. "I'm gonna go out for a while, okay?" he said.

"Are you sure you're okay, son?"

"I'm all right. I just want to be by my own self. I'll be here for dinner."

"Me too," I said, lying on the bed with my forearm covering my eyes. Monty went out, just blowing off the grounding I gave him. Then Ma left too, but not before leaving us a long *Hmmmm* to let us know she noticed.

I woke up just before dinner. When I walked into the kitchen, Ma was holding Monty's chin in her hand. I got a shiver. It was a scene I'd walked in on before, my mother cradling a damaged face in her hands.

"I didn't notice that was loose before," she said, looking into his mouth.

"Oh ya," he answered, "I've been twisting it around in there for weeks."

He left the house with two eye teeth, came back with one.

My Job

The night before we were to meet the Big Brother character, Ma came into our room to make the final pitch. It seemed like every minute she was a little more sure that everything would be great if Monty and I would just buddy up with old—I can hardly say it—Chaz.

Monty was reading a book when she came in, *Ten Days to Tremendous Triceps*. He slapped his book shut and squeezed it between flat palms, to flex. "Bring him on, Ma," he said. "We'll take on all challengers."

I couldn't believe what was happening. It was as if he knew just what to say to make Ma believe he was beyond redemption, that he needed outside help.

"It's not *your* aggression I'm worried about at the moment, Monty," she said, staring me down.

"Ma, I said I would give the guy a chance," I

119

said, though I know nobody in the room bought it.

"You'll see, George," she said. "Chaz is a fine man. You'll like him." Every time she said his name, it was like she lowered a big bell over my head and gonged it.

I "uh-huhed" a few times and she left, a little disappointed with me but still determined that this was going to happen. After I killed the light and tried to sleep, Monty started tormenting me. He'd gotten unreal by that time, the way he could sense exactly how to stick me.

"Chaz . . . Chaz . . . Chaz," he chanted quietly, out of the side of his mouth, sounding like the Penguin in *Batman*.

"Ya, Chaz . . . Chaaaaz . . . Chaz."

On Saturday morning I got home from my route at eight. I was kind of torn—all antsy and wired up, but not wanting to leave my room. So I cleaned up. Monty was out of the room before I got home.

"What are you doing?" he said as he came back in.

"I'm straightening up," I said. "This place is a pit."

Monty shook his head at me. "Boring, George. Boring, boring, boring. I wouldn't do it unless I was getting paid. A lot."

"That's because you're irresponsible," I told him.

That made him laugh. "Listen," he said, "Chaz is here."

GONG.

"How does he look?"

"He looks like a museum guy. God, I hope he's not a museum guy. I don't want to spend my Saturday in a museum."

I grunted.

Monty shrugged and walked back toward the door. "Anyway, you better get out there. And you better stop being nutty. Ma's already saying you better not act nutty today."

When I got to the kitchen, Chaz was sitting at the kitchen table, in *my* chair, having coffee with Ma. He spun around.

"Hey, sport, I've been waiting to meet you. We've got places to go. Lots to do," Chaz said, clapping his hands and rubbing them together.

"I've been working," I said to him. "I'm a very busy man." I left the room.

"George, come back here," Ma called. "What's the matter with you?"

"I heard the toilet running. I was going to go jiggle it."

"Well jiggle it later. Come over here and meet

our guest, please," Ma said.

"Don't mind him, Chaz," Monty said. "He's always in the bathroom jiggling it." Monty laughed. Chaz laughed.

"I'll jiggle your little neck," I said. Ma was totally unamused, but she just turned red quietly, which meant she was filing it away for later.

"Hey," Chaz said. "It's cool, I was thirteen years old once."

I stuck out my hand and squeezed Chaz's as hard as I could. "Fourteen. I'm not thirteen, I'm fourteen. He's not thirteen either," I said, pointing at Monty without looking at him. "And he might never get there." I kept squeezing his hand, getting no reaction until suddenly he started squeezing back. Hard. I tried to let go, but he wouldn't let me. He just kept shaking, smiling, squeezing, until I could feel the bones in my hand crackling. He did it so smoothly that nobody else could tell what he was doing, and I couldn't let them see. When my eyes started to water, he let go.

"Good grip." Chaz laughed. He chucked me on the chin like a little boy. I wanted to chuck him in the groin.

Ma crossed her arms and smiled at us, like she thought we were having a good time. "Well, Chaz, I think I should tell you that at first George didn't think that this was such a great idea."

"Oh no?" Chaz's chin stuck way out when he laughed. "Oh well, I think we can turn old Georgie around."

"Ya, let's turn him around," Monty said. "What are we gonna do?"

"What do you like to do?" Chaz said.

"I like to eat, and do sports, and go to R-rated movies, and sit on benches at the park, dropping bread on the ground in front of my feet so I can try to punt the pigeons."

"We'll do that, then," Chaz said happily.

"Ah . . ." Ma interrupted.

"We'll do *some* of that, then. How 'bout you, George old man? What do you like to do on a Saturday?"

"I like to sleep late, like till seven. Then I do my route, then I clean my room. Then, if Monty and me have any jobs lined up—we do a lot of paid work for people—then we go and do that. If I'm really tired, I take a nap in the afternoon or I watch a Bruins game. When I'm not doing that stuff, I like to be by myself."

Chaz smiled at me. Then he looked at Ma. She shrugged. "George is having a bit of a spell at the moment," she said. Then she looked at me, making her eyebrows into a sharp V. "But he'll be more himself starting now, I *promise*."

"I'm not worried," Chaz said. "I'm sure George is a very fun person once you get to know him."

"I think you're gonna be disappointed," Monty said.

We walked down the stairs as Chaz finished laying everything out for Ma. "Give the guy a chance, George," Monty said. "What do you want to get rid of him for anyway?"

"We just don't need him, that's all. You gonna help me get rid of him?"

Monty thought about it. "No. I want to see what he's got."

"Suit yourself," I said.

Chaz caught up to us near the bottom of the stairs, passing right by us, then turning to face us from the bottom landing.

"Where are we going?" I asked.

Chaz smiled up at us. "Well, it's sort of a museum."

Monty leaned and whispered in my ear, "Okay, how do you want to get rid of him?"

I sat in the front seat of Chaz's car, an old Plymouth Duster. Monty sat in back. "Seventy-five?" I asked.

"Very good," Chaz answered. He turned the key and the engine cranked with a loud *bub-bub-*

bub sound, like a tugboat.

"You need a new manifold," I said. "So you don't have any money then, huh?"

"Not much." He laughed. I sat sideways on the seat, so I could see both him and Monty. Chaz adjusted the rearview mirror, and Monty waved at him in it.

"So, this is your first trip to the Basketball Hall of Fame?" Chaz said.

"Springfield?" Monty leaned over the front seat. "Awesome. You tricked us—that's not a museum."

"Sure it is," Chaz said. "It's really just around the corner. I'm surprised you guys haven't been there before."

"We were going to go when I get my license," I said.

"I'm sorry, George," Chaz said. "I don't want to spoil it. We could do something else."

"No way," Monty said. "By the time George is driving, there'll be fifty million new players in there, so we can go again."

"Great. Then just sit back and enjoy the ride. It'll take about a half hour, but we can get to know each other better on the way. George, why don't you start. Tell me something about yourself."

"I get carsick."

"Okay. How about you, Monty?"

"I get carsick, but only if I don't get to stop on the way for something to eat. Meat." We'd barely pulled from the curb when Monty started yelling at Chaz, "Whoa, whoa, stop."

Chaz pulled over and Monty threw the door open. In stepped the silent, increasingly somber Fred the Head, wearing his tam.

"Hope you don't mind," Monty said. "This is my sidekick, Fred. He won't be any trouble, and I'm kind of his big brother."

Chaz turned to me and I nodded.

"Now tell us about you, Chaz." I said as we started off again. "Are you married? What do you do for work? Do you have a family? Do you have a life? What are you doing this for?"

"Fair enough, George. I don't have a wife, but I do have a very nice girlfriend I've been seeing for a long time—"

"Is she big?" Monty interrupted. I gave him a stare.

"She's . . . average size," Chaz said, trying to get a look at Monty in the mirror. "And I work for the government—"

"What color hair does she have?" Monty cut him off again.

Chaz laughed out loud and adjusted the mirror

to find Monty, who was scrunched way down in the seat, admiring his own biceps and letting Fred feel them. "That's right, you're in sixth grade, aren't you? She's got blond hair and I don't want to talk about her anymore right now."

"Ya, shut up," I said.

"I work for the census bureau—I work on statistics. I have a family, but they live in other parts of the country mostly. And to answer the big question, I am a Big Brother because I want to work with kids who need someone like me in their lives. I add something different to their lives, and they do the same for me."

"Well, maybe we're not the guys you're looking for, 'cause we don't need someone like you," I said. "No offense. Hey, maybe Fred there is interested."

Monty whistled from the backseat. "It's a good thing Ma isn't here."

"No, that's okay. I'm aware that George isn't thrilled with this arrangement yet. It's fine if you tell me what's on your mind. I appreciate your honesty, George. But I do wish you'd give me a chance."

"I'm going to. Ma wants me to."

We didn't do a whole lot more talking before we stopped for something to eat. I looked out the window, then at Chaz, without letting him see. He stared at the road ahead, gripping the wheel tightly with both hands and smiling a forced smile. Monty nodded off. Fred just stared out the window, vigilant, like a pointy-headed owl. We pulled into a McDonald's.

"This okay with you, Monty?" Chaz said.

"Huh? Huh?" Monty was slow to wake up.

"Why are you pulling into the parking lot?" I asked. "Let's just go through the drive-through, it'll be quicker."

"Sure." Monty caught up. "McDonald's is fine with me."

"Relax, George, we're in no great rush. Let's sit down and eat." Chaz put his hand on my shoulder as he put the car in park. I stared at the hand until he pulled it away.

Monty had scrambled eggs, hash browns, two sausage patties, and a danish. The danish was originally Fred's, but he showed no interest. Whenever Monty gets taken out to eat, he feels like he has to eat like an animal. Chaz and I both had just coffee, but he took two sugars.

"Look at this," Monty said, holding up the solid mass of egg in one hand and the sausage in the other. "Same shape." They were both shaped like the sole of a small shoe, until Monty took a bite from each. Then he picked up the hash browns and danish, holding them up side by side. "They're *all* the same shape," he said. "*This* is great food. I don't understand why Ma won't let us eat here."

Chaz had been smiling at everything Monty said, but now he got nervous. "What?" He leaned over the table toward Monty. Then he turned to me, sitting beside him. "Your mother doesn't allow you to eat at McDonald's?"

I took a sip from my coffee. "She said if we ever ate here, she'd pump our stomachs with a fire hose."

Chaz shook his head. He held his hands out to me, palms up, and said, "George . . . ?"

"I think their coffee is quite good," I said. I sipped. Monty paid no attention to any of this.

"Do they serve hot apple pies with the breakfast food? Or do you have to wait till later?" Monty said.

I thought for sure that Chaz would get a little mad by now, but he started laughing again. "All right, you guys," he said. "I can see how it's going to be."

"You don't need to worry, Chaz," I said. "You don't have to get into trouble. If you want to *lie* to our mother, we won't tell on you. Will we, Monty?"

"Can I get a pie?"

Chaz threw me by laughing even harder. He could roll with some punches, I had to give him that. "Get in the car. There will be no lying to your mother. By anyone." Monty started laughing, too, but I don't think he even knew why. When Chaz put his arm around Monty's shoulder on the way out, Monty put his arm around Chaz's back and his other arm around my shoulder. It felt kind of fun as we walked like that through the parking lot for a few steps, but then I had to knock his hand down. As I dropped back, I bumped into Fred, and as I turned I noticed he had a shaken look on his face. He'd been giving Chaz some hairy looks already, but when he touched Monty, it was too much.

The Head scurried up behind them and grabbed Monty's arm. When Monty looked at him, he just shook his head in a kind of urgent no.

"Sorry, man," Monty said to Chaz. "But I have to take care of my boy." He put his arm around Fred, who gave Chaz a look like he wanted to fight.

"Have you been here before?" Monty asked as we neared the Hall.

"Yes," Chaz said. "But it's been a few years. It's a great place for sports fans like you guys."

"I always wanted to see it," Monty said.

"Why didn't you tell me?" I'd never heard him mention it once. "I could have brought you."

"Right. On your bike?" Monty said. Chaz laughed but tried to cover his mouth, as if he could take it back.

"I'd appreciate it if you laugh at him only when he says something funny."

"I apologize, George, I didn't mean to laugh."

Monty leaned forward and said, low but not whispering, into Chaz's ear, "See. I tried to tell you he was not a fun guy."

"Oh, I don't agree with that at all," Chaz said. "I think there's a lot of fun in George. And we're going to bring it out."

I looked at him out of the corner of my eye. He was doing a lot of nodding and driving with his elbows way up in the air, happy style.

Monty threw himself back in the seat again. "Okay," he said. "You'll see."

When we were finally inside the Hall, Chaz led us around, giving little speeches, like he was a tour guide. Monty hung on everything Chaz said.

"Nobody played Jabbar tougher than Dave Cowens did," Chaz said as they stood in front of Cowens's plaque.

"Hakeem Olajuwan did," I said.

131

"Ya, but that was when Kareem was old," Chaz responded.

"Bob Lanier did," I said.

"Say, you go pretty far back, young man." He made his eyes really wide to act impressed. "You know Bob Lanier. Biggest feet on the planet."

"Bill Walton played him tougher than Cowens did, too."

Monty tapped Chaz on the arm. "He reads a lot of sports books," he said, pointing at me.

"How old are you, Chaz?" I asked while we passed through the Builders section of the Hall, where they honor owners and league presidents, the section where even the adults seemed bored.

"I'm thirty-one years old."

"Do you think that the game was better back in your day?"

He laughed. "My day?"

"Of course the game was better then," Monty jumped in. "All old guys say all games were always better before we came along."

"No, now wait a minute. That's not entirely true. I think that baseball used to be better. Hockey and football never really change much. But basketball? I find it hard to imagine that basketball ever has been or ever will be played any better than it's being played right now. You guys

132

are lucky, growing up watching Michael Jordan, Magic Johnson, Larry Bird . . ."

The four of us sat down on a stone bench in a big circular room. "I notice you didn't mention any centers," I said.

"True, true. But Ewing is excellent when he's motivated. Olajuwan, David Robinson, Shaquille O'Neal . . ."

"But no Bill Russells, or Chamberlains," I said, pointing a finger at Chaz, who nodded.

"True enough," he said.

"Charles Barkley is the best player of all time," Monty challenged, standing up on the bench. Fred climbed up beside him, for moral support, I suppose.

"You don't know anything," I said. "Sit down. Chaz, listen to this. Bill Russell at center. John Havlicek and Doctor J. at forward. Oscar Robertson and Bob Cousy at guard. That's my team to beat anyone."

"Wow," Chaz said. "Tough team to beat, no doubt about it. But to tell you the truth, George, I think a lot of players get better in people's minds after they've been gone for a long time. I wouldn't be surprised if a team of players who are active right now could beat that one."

"Players today don't have the determination,

the intangibles, of the old-timers," I told him. He shook his head, smiling.

"You're a pretty nostalgic fifteen-year-old," he said.

"I'm fourteen." I smiled, even though I was pretty sure he made the mistake on purpose.

"Charles Barkley, Karl Malone, Charles Oakley, Shaq, and Larry Johnson," Monty blurted. "That's my team."

"What's that, Monty, the All-Steroids team? You got nothing but monsters on that team. If you were trying to get a wrestlemania team together, I could see it. . . ."

"Well, that's my team. They'd kick the hell out of *yours*."

"And it's a fine team," Chaz said. Monty smiled and nodded at me, then back up at Chaz. He's got some decent moves, I thought, as Chaz threw a few fake jabs at me, then Monty. But when they tried to include Fred, the poor little squirrel jumped like Chaz had pulled a gun on him. Even *I* didn't hate the guy that much.

"So you think I need to get my manifold fixed, huh, George?" Chaz said as we neared home.

"Ya, maybe pipes too."

"Where'd you learn about cars?"

"A guy we do some work for has a garage. I go over there when I can, to learn, but Ma hates his guts, and I don't like to hang out places she doesn't care for. *So I don't go there very much*," I said, turning to Monty.

"What's a manifold, Chaz?" Monty asked, hanging over the front seat again, missing the point of my story.

"Your brother could tell you better than I could."

"Okay, tell me later, George. Chaz, what kind of statistics do you do at work? Does your girl-friend have a job, or is she just, like, a girl?"

We pulled up in front of Fred's house before Chaz could answer him. "We'll pick it up next time, buddy," Chaz said, sticking his hand out over his shoulder for Monty to slap it, which he did. By the time he extended his palm to the Head, he was gone, like he'd slipped out the open window or something. Monty got out with him, calling back from the front stairs.

"Thanks, buddy. Next week you can ask *me* some questions if you want."

"I will," Chaz said. I stared at Monty waving like a little kid from the stairs. As Chaz drove on to drop me at our building, he got really warm with me.

"George, I had a great time with you guys today. Ask your mother if she could give me a call when she gets home from work, will you? And about next week. I thought we'd go to the auto show." Chaz smiled big at that.

I got out in front of our place and walked around to the driver-side window. I stood straight and folded my arms across my chest. I looked away from Chaz, up and down the street, before I answered him.

"Maybe not, Chaz. Maybe you just shouldn't come back. I mean, you are a nice guy, and we had a good time, but . . . like I said before, we don't need you. You should spend your time with some kids who do, don't you think? And please, don't think you'll get me to work through this. I guarantee I won't let this thing work. Sorry."

I looked down at him. His mouth hung open and his eyes were round. "Please, when you talk to Ma, just tell her that we didn't get along," I said. "She'll know it was me." I turned away and ran up the stairs without looking at Chaz again.

It didn't feel too great, chasing Chaz off. Monty wasn't going to like it. Ma sure wasn't going to like it. But I just couldn't let it happen. Monty was mine to take care of, and I couldn't just give him up. Not yet.

11

The Willies

Even after all this time I still like to be up early, crack of dawn if I can, and doing something alone. Most mornings I'm sitting on the step when the truck comes by with my papers, then he's gone and I have the daybreak to myself again. That time of day is all mine. But for a while Herbie changed all that.

"For a really smart kid Fred doesn't know a lot of very simple things," Mary B. said to me, talking about her brother, the Head. It was six thirty in the morning, and she had just popped up talking away at me while I delivered my papers.

"Is that right, Mary?" I said, not knowing how to talk to a kid like this. She did try hard, though, a lot harder than her brother did. Sometimes, like this morning, she would go all day without her quadruplefocal glasses just so that she could be regular for a while. When she wore them, looking at her was like looking into kaleidoscopes. When she didn't wear them, she looked like she was staring straight into the sun, and she walked with her hands out in front of her.

"It's all right, you can call me Herbie."

"Great," I said, sky-hooking a paper onto a second-floor porch. "What are you doing here, Herbie?"

"Nothing," she said. "Just walking around. I like to get out of the house as much as I can, don't you? Usually I'm out long before you deliver your papers. I know that because I check the houses where you deliver, and they don't have their papers yet. I'm a little sluggish this morning, and that's why I'm late. But I guess it's not too bad, because most mornings I just walk around the neighborhood by myself or with the dogs that are always running around here loose, but today I can walk with you."

"That's nice," I said, but it was a good thing she couldn't see my face. She walked along with me the whole route, chirping away like a little bird all the way. It was difficult at first, but it got to be not so bad to listen to. And she was more than happy to help me out, taking care of all the difficult customers who wanted their papers inside the screen door, or on the back porch, or under the mat, or on a shelf in the garage. She freed me up to fire away with the plain old front-porch deliveries, so the route took half the time it usually did.

"Buy you a cup of coffee?" Herbie said to me when we finished at ten of seven. We were right near the coffee shop. "I understand you're big on java."

"Huh? Ya, well it's something I'm working on." Now she had me not only surprised but nervous. I looked up and down the street to see if anyone was around, but it was early enough for me to be safe. Herbie was a good kid, and she did help me out, so it was the least I could do. But if anyone I knew witnessed this scene, I would be today's Big Joke of the Playground.

"All right," I said. "But a very quick one. And I'll do the buying."

Of course she was there waiting for me the next morning. And the next. I tried staggering my starting times, but she must have watched out her window for me to come down, because she always made the adjustments. But it would be a lie to say it was all bad. I wound up paying her fifty cents a day to do the special deliveries. It wasn't much, but she only had to deliver ten papers and she would have been up anyway, roaming around with the dogs. I would have paid her twice as much to stay home. Not because she wasn't nice to have around, but for how nervous it made me that my friends would see this and bust me until I was dead. I got to like her a lot, to be honest.

Monty had an afternoon route, and he tried to hire Herbie to go with him, but she wasn't interested. The Head always went with Monty, but he wasn't helpful the way his sister was. Herbie said work was not hard for her because her job around the house was *every* job, while Fred's job was to stay out of the way and keep his head out of the windows. She said her father told her, "As long as you're going to look like a donkey, you might as well work like one." She didn't seem to mind all that much when she told me this, although it was sometimes tough to tell her smile from her wince. On Sundays, when everybody delivers morning papers, we all traveled together, me with Herbie and Monty with Fred.

Everyone got pretty comfortable with the arrangement of having the Rafkins around, even if it wasn't something we bragged about at school. All through the winter Herbie was possibly the most reliable paper person I ever saw, except for a few absences that she never explained, but that always happened on days when her father's cab stayed in front of the house all day. But when the weather started to turn warmer, in March, she be-gan missing our mornings more often, and she and Fred would be out of school. The following day she would be back at work chattering on like nothing had happened, but the Head, Monty said, didn't bounce back the same way.

"Fred's getting funnier," he told me on one of the rare mornings in March when we walked alone to school. "You know how he never liked to say too much anyway? Well, these days he barely ever says a word, even to me."

"Maybe he doesn't like you anymore," I said. "That would be rough, if even Fred the Head doesn't want to hang with you."

"No, that's not it," he said. "I think he likes me even more, the less he says. Wherever I go, he hangs right by my shoulder, making every move I make. Like he's afraid I'm gonna lose him or some-thing. I almost feel like he wants to touch me, you know? To reach out and hang on to my shoulders. I never saw such a scared kid before, George. I've kind of had to become his guardian angel."

"Time out. What's that mean?"

"Four times in the last two weeks, I've had to take guys outside for hassling my boy."

"Whoa. *Four* times, Monty?"

"Don't worry about it, George, I don't *lose*."

"That's not the point. I think maybe you're getting a little punch happy."

"George, I do what is right. He needs me. There are those of us who *can* and those who *cannot*. I happen to be a can, that's all. And Fred, well . . . you know." When Monty saw I wasn't exactly moved by this explanation, he had a sudden urge to get all righteous and somber. "Their cat finally died, you know."

"It starved to death, right?"

"They don't know for sure. The kids came home from school one day and the cat was gone. The Willies told them that the cat went to California. He thought that was funny."

On April Fools' Day, the Rafkin kids were late to school. The report was that their father was shot. Everybody thought it was a joke, but it turned out to be true. Herbie told me the next morning as if it was nothing special.

"He took one in the shoulder, a fleshy part. This is the third time. Cab driving is just such a dangerous job."

Being a cold-blooded bastard is a dangerous job too, I thought, but I didn't share it with her. "Poor guy" was what I actually said.

"Yes, it is a bad thing," Herbie said. She sounded as if she meant it even less than I did. "I won't be going to school today. I have to take care of things at home."

I was surprised not only at how calm she was, but that, at nine years old, decisions like this were hers to make.

"Well, Herbie, you didn't have to come to work this morning either. I would have understood."

"Oh no, I wanted to. Besides, he's not awake yet, so it's okay."

When Monty and I passed by the house on the way to school, Fred didn't come out to meet us like he usually did. We figured he was staying home too, but actually he was already gone. I didn't know anything about it until that night. Monty stayed out all afternoon after school. He was with Fred. His papers sat in a bundle on the porch undelivered. By the time he came in, Ma and I were sitting at the supper table. She was worried, but making it sound like she was mad. She demanded that I tell her where he was, as if I knew.

"If he's at the Willies' house, I want you to tell me, George." They didn't have a phone, so she couldn't call to check and she didn't want to go there unless she absolutely had to.

"No, Ma. He doesn't go there. He never even

143

gets invited to go there anymore."

"Good. That is a bad man over there. I'm sure whoever shot him had to stand in line to do it. George, where is your brother?"

Just then, Monty walked in. Fred the Head walked in three inches behind him. Ma had her mouth wide open, ready to unload on Monty, when the Head peeked around him.

Both his eyes were black. He had masking tape holding his glasses together in the middle and on one hinge, but it was coming apart. His top lip was puffed up and oozing like a garden slug, with a wide crack in the middle. Fred had taken more than a few slappings in the school yard, but that wasn't what we had here. He told them at school that he was in a car accident. But we knew who the accident was.

"Mum," Monty said. Whenever he called her that, it meant he was feeling really like a kid. "Mum, we have company for dinner, okay?"

I could see her trying to hold it together, because that was her job. "Sure. Of course, Monty. Fred, it is nice to see you again." Fred didn't respond. I could feel my mouth hanging open, so I closed it. Fred was hard to look at. Not hard the way he was always hard to look at, but hard like it made your eyes water. We all acted a lot like Fred at dinner. Nobody talked. Ma tried a couple of times to start something, but it wouldn't come. The meal took forty minutes or so but it seemed like a month. Nobody ate much either. The meat loaf was something special, and there was a ton of it because Monty and me are such pigs about it, but it pretty much sat there while we all picked. Fred ate a few peas and that was it. That may have been because of his lip, but he was never too hot for food anyway.

Without warning, Fred jumped up from the table as if he had to answer the phone.

"Why don't you kick back for a while?" Monty said, standing up too. Fred just shook his head. He had to go and we knew it. He went over and shook my mother's hand. She took it, and held it for a few seconds between her hands.

"You know, Fred, you can stay over if you like," she said. Again he shook his head. Ma reached out and held that head, touching all his hurt places lightly with her fingertips. Tears came from her eyes, but Fred didn't cry. "Thank you for dinner; I have to be going." He didn't say anything more when Monty walked him out.

When Monty came back to the table, his eyes were all red. He threw himself down in his chair.

"We have to do something," he screamed,

smashing his open hands down on the table.

"What can we do?" I said.

"Let's kick his ass, Georgie." Monty jumped back to his feet, yelled it louder, "Kick his ass. You and me can do it."

"Stop it! Now stop it. Monty, I want you to stop talking crazy right this minute," Ma said. "You want to get yourself killed? You just can't do things that way. Don't you ever, ever let me hear you talk about trying to settle things with violence." She wiped the tears from her face, going from sad to forceful with the wipe of her hand. She got up and marched to the phone.

Monty turned to me and whispered, "Come on, George, help me."

"Help you what?" I grabbed his shoulder with one hand and shook his skinny body all around. "Help you die? Ma's right, Monty—the guy will have us for lunch, then pick his teeth with Herbie and Fred." I thought about Herbie. "Let Ma handle it."

"Oh ya," Monty said, leering maniacally, like he was pulling out the ultimate gun. "Well, maybe I'll just get my uncle Archie to break the Willies' goddamn neck."

By now he had me scared. I honestly didn't know what he'd say or do next. I leaned in close while Ma had her back to us, and I grabbed him by the neck. By the throat, really. "Not . . . another . . . word," I growled before he slapped my hand away. I kept one eye on Ma.

She called the Department of Social Services. Ma works for the State Rehabilitation Commission and she knows how to talk to agencies. She told them loudly, using her most serious work words, what a deviant type of abusive, negligent, dysfunctional, psychotic boozer the Willies was, although no, she had not witnessed any incidents. That seemed to be a big sticking point. They told her that they were looking into it and that in fact the nuns had already called on this.

"That's all we can do for now. We let the system work," Ma told us when she got off the phone. Monty stormed toward the bedroom, punched the door. "Monty," she said to him, "do not do anything more. Do you understand me?" He went into the room without responding. "George, keep an eye on him the next few days," she said. "I think you understand things a little better. And try to keep an eye on those poor Rafkin children if you can. From a distance." She kept running both hands back over her forehead and through her hair nervously.

I said I would, even though I didn't know what

I was supposed to be doing. I like responsibility, but sometimes I feel like I've got more than I truly know what to do with.

I went to bed early. Monty was already asleep. I started thinking about Herbie again. I kept waking up during the night. When I went out a little early to start my route, Herbie was waiting for me on my steps. She had her glasses on. I looked closely at her and noticed a red patch on her cheek just below the left lens. I saw my hand shaking when I reached out and lifted the glasses up over her eyes.

The skin on the outside of her eye was all purple and yellow, with a high shine. Inside, from the light-blue part out to the corner, the part of Herbie's eyeball that was supposed to be white was entirely red, blood, like it had just been painted.

"George, I'm not going to be working today," she said as she pulled her face away from my hand. "I hope you don't mind, but I wanted to tell you. I'm going home now, good-bye."

"I'm going with you," I said.

"No. You can't," she said.

"Then come up to our place, and bring Fred too."

"No, don't worry about it," she said. "Fred and I know what to do. We'll be okay." She smiled and turned to go. Then she turned back. "But I do like that you want to help." She hesitated, then ran back to me, throwing her arms around my neck and kissing my cheek. Just as quickly, she ran off again.

My route took three times as long as it did when Herbie was with me. Even longer than when I used to do it alone all the time. When I got home, it was late, time to go to school. Monty was waiting for me with my books in his hand. When we got to the Rafkins' house, there was nobody waiting to walk with us. They were staying out of school again. I tried to treat it like all the other times—I was supposed to understand things better than Monty—but I couldn't.

This was one of those times when we both didn't understand nothin'.

I stopped on the sidewalk in front of the house and stood there. I looked up at the second floor, where they lived, but I couldn't see anything. My whole body was shaking.

"Monty," I said while I was still looking up at the windows, "let's go."

The words weren't out of my mouth before we'd dumped all our books on the sidewalk and Monty was up the stairs ahead of me with a baseball-size rock in each hand. I carried a brick, but I don't know how or where I got it. I had no idea what we were trying to do by running up there, other than getting ourselves a good beating.

We pushed open the outside door, which was always unlocked, and opened the inside door. The two of us flew up the stairs, tripping and climbing over each other so that we couldn't have surprised anyone, and when we crashed into the apartment we found nothing.

In the living room there were two wicker outdoor chairs and nothing else. In the dining room one gray metal folding chair. We stood there looking around silently for a few seconds.

"How did they get everything out so fast?" I asked as I looked out the front window. I hadn't noticed before that the cab was gone.

"This is all they ever *had*," Monty screamed. Then he fired his rocks through two windows.

12

Every Man for Himself

I was sitting on Monty's back on Saturday starting at one fifteen in the afternoon. That's the only place we would ever be during hockey season when the Bruins were playing a Saturday matinee. Monty lay down flat on the rug in front of the TV and I sat on his back. The only one other place of course we would ever be on a Saturday that the Bruins were playing would be at the Garden. But Ma says that all the beer-belly deviates there would just spoil the game for us. She's very sour on the Garden, on arenas.

Mostly, it can be a fun deal to watch the game the way Monty and I do anyway. Hockey can get pretty rough, and we're participatory-type guys. So when there is a hard check or a fight—especially when there's a fight—or when the referee blows a

151

call like he does every thirty seconds or so, I traditionally take it out on Monty's back. He's a skinny guy, but when you pound his chest or his back, it sounds like he's hollow, like banging on the bottom of a plastic trash barrel. Even he thinks it's funny.

This one Saturday, though, something had changed. I was really tattooing him, and he didn't do anything. He didn't even lean on his elbows with his chin in his hands, like usual; he lay facedown on the rug. It was eerie the way his body just lay there while I beat the bejesus out of it for the whole first period. Not even a grunt. Acted like I didn't even bother him.

"What's the matter with you?" I asked him between periods.

"Nothing," he said without even taking his face off the rug.

"These are the Bruins and Canadiens here. Adams Division Finals. Something's got to be wrong."

"Why should I tell you?" he said.

"So something *is* the matter." I knocked on his head like a door.

"Just leave me alone, will ya, George?"

"Don't be mysterious, Monty. If there's something wrong, you know you can tell me."

Monty looked back at me over his shoulder even though all he could turn was his head with me sitting on him. "Oh I can, can I? Can I really talk to you, George?" He was looking at me hard, shooting lasers through me with his eyes. I wasn't sure what he was getting at, but it was pretty clear he had some kind of problem with me. I backed off.

The Bruins and Canadiens came back out onto the ice and skated in circles for a while. Monty and I sat quietly for a bit. It felt like we were waiting for something.

"I got a wicked case for Linda O'Leary," he yelled out of nowhere into the rug. It sounded like it hurt.

I turned his head sideways so his mouth was off the rug. "Say that again?" I said.

"No." He turned over so that I rolled off his back. I just lay there on the floor looking at him while he stomped over and sat on the love seat. He folded his arms and pretended to watch the game without me.

"Mrs. O'Leary's cow? Monty, you like Mrs. O'Leary's cow? Boy, you get next to her and you'll be giving new meaning to the phrase 'doing the nasty.'"

"Shut up, George."

"That's one 'shut up' today, Monty. Two more and—"

"Shut up shut up shut up shut up shut up shut up!"

I couldn't believe this. This just didn't happen. A week's worth of shut ups in one breath. Things were just not the way they were supposed to be.

I tried to help him see things straight. "What are you, mental or something? You don't want to watch the Bruins and Canadiens, you lie with your face on the floor, you don't talk. Jeez, Monty, this is Saturday. *Saturday*. And then you risk your life giving me lip. And why? All this just because of horsy face?"

I swear, I never saw him put his feet on the floor when he jumped on me. He must have pushed off entirely with his butt muscles. And he flew. Off the couch, over the coffee table, and right onto my chest.

"All right!" I said as we rolled around the floor. "That's more like it." It was a great fight. Our mother works on Saturdays. We crashed into everything in the living room except the TV. We tipped over the coffee table and kicked Ma's stuffed reading chair across the floor until it got jammed in the doorway. Then I realized this was no hockey fight. There were no air punches, we didn't pull each other's shirts over our heads, we didn't skate around the floor in our socks and pretend to drop our gloves. There were always a few punches that landed by accident even in hockey fights, but when Monty caught me with a clean uppercut on that sharp bone just above the eye, it dawned on me that he'd hit me in the head ten times already, and he was coming back for more.

I had no choice but to put a stop to it. But when I stepped toward him, he stepped up too. He leaned his head into mine, then quickly jumped back and snuck up *another* chin chuck. I never taught him that!

"All right now, Monty, that's enough," I said when I headlocked him. For his size, he has a very big head, and it takes a good grip. He squirmed and tried to lift me on his shoulder, almost managing it. Instead he started hammering me with kidney punches.

"Okay, I'm trying to make it easy on you, but if that's the way you want it—" I said. Then I bent over, with him still in the headlock, and rolled him over my hip. His whole body flew over like a rag doll in fast motion, his feet coming down last. I landed on top of him just right. Monty was on his back, I was lying across his chest, and he was still in that headlock. If I'd pulled that off when we were playing Superstars of Wrestling, it would have been spectacular. But Monty was mad and taking the zing out of everything.

He was being really quiet lying there, pretending again to be watching the Bruins game, like I would fall for that.

"I'm gonna let you up now, Monty, so don't go scud on me again, okay? Okay?"

He wouldn't say anything, and usually that means he's not going to cooperate. But I let him go anyway.

I didn't even have my arm off his head for two seconds before he grabbed it and sank his teeth in. "Ahhhhh!" I yelled, and shook my arm all over. But he was like a shark and wouldn't let go. I took my other hand and punched him straight in the forehead. He let go and fell back on the floor. There were already three knuckle marks showing up in the middle of his head, but that was okay because I had teethmarks to show if he tried to take this over my head to Ma.

I don't shock easy, but I was shocked when he started getting up after me like one of those *Night of the Living Dead* creatures that wouldn't die.

"All right, that's it," I said. I flipped him back to the floor and put him on the rug, which was nowhere near where it was when we started. Then

I rolled him up in it. It's only a five by seven, so I had to roll him up lengthwise, but he was in there good and tight. Then I sat on him to watch the game.

But it wasn't any fun. The Bruins were winning 3–0, and I hate the Canadiens more than anything except, naturally, the New York Rangers, Yankees, Mets, Giants, Jets, and Knicks. But I couldn't get into it. Monty wouldn't watch. He just lay there mumbling, "Don't you ever say that again" and "I'll kick your butt" and other worse stuff that got even tougher to ignore. So finally, for everybody's sake, I picked him up, still all rolled up, and carried him to the hallway. I pushed Ma's chair out of the way, stepped into the hall, which has no carpeting, and as hard as I could, I slid him down the hall toward the kitchen. That hallway has the slickest floor (it's where we usually play sock hockey), and Monty looked kind of cool, sliding toward the kitchen like a giant sausage. When he bumped to a stop at the kitchen threshold, he didn't move or talk.

"And don't come back in here till you fix your attitude," I yelled. "It's Saturday. You're ruining Saturday, Monty. And for what?"

"Don't say it," he yelled back.

He didn't scare me, of course, but I didn't say it

157

anyway. To tell the truth, I was in no rush to go at it with him again. But without him, even with the Bruins, the afternoon was one big dead zone.

When Ma got home at around four thirty, I was vacuuming. When she saw me, she looked all around, really suspicious like, with her hands on her hips. She's very pretty, I happened to notice right then.

"George? It is Saturday, you know. What are you doing?"

"I'm cleaning up, Ma. It was kind of messy around here. No offense."

"No, certainly not, no offense taken. Son, anytime you find the condition of this apartment distasteful, I don't want you to be bashful at all about cleaning it up. It's just a bit unusual, that's all, since it's a nice Saturday and everything. Why aren't you guys outside? And where is Monty anyway?"

It was a while earlier that I had gone down the hall and found the rug empty but still all rolled up just like I'd left it. Monty is like a Houdini, the way he can collapse his shoulders, his ribs, practically his whole body except for that head, when he wants to get out of something. He usually doesn't even have to make up his bed after he slithers out of it in the morning. The covers just stay all neat like they were before he got in.

"I think he's in our room."

"You think? George, there are four rooms in this apartment. You don't know which one your brother is in?"

"Ya, he's in the bedroom. He's being weird today."

"He's not the only one. Go ahead, don't let me interrupt your housework."

I finished the vacuuming and went around the place with a feather duster while Ma went in to talk to Monty. The housework stuff wasn't so bad, but Ma was right, it was no way to spend a Saturday.

I waited for her at the kitchen table. When she came out with a little smile on her face, I stopped pinching my bite mark to make it look worse in case I needed it.

"You're right, George, he is feeling a little strange, I think. But it isn't anything too serious." She kicked off her shoes.

"Women," I said.

"Yes, women," she said.

We both nodded. "Want to split a ginger ale with me?" I asked her.

Ma's chair was up against a wall. She leaned her head back against the shiny wood paneling. "Yes, son, that sounds like a wonderful idea." We sat together and sipped.

"The house is nice and clean, George—thank

you. That saves me a lot of time."

"I was happy to do it, Ma." I threw my arm over the back of my chair and leaned on the back two legs. Ma doesn't like it when we do that, but sometimes when it's just the two of us at the table like this, she doesn't say anything about it.

"But didn't the two of you get outside at all today? It was such a nice day."

I pointed out the kitchen door toward my bedroom. "*He* wouldn't do anything today. He wouldn't go out, he wouldn't play any games, he wouldn't do any work. He wouldn't even watch the Bruins and Canadiens. I couldn't even talk to him, Ma."

"Well, George. Just because *he* didn't want to go out, did that mean that *you* couldn't go out?"

"Huh?"

"Yes, you could just go out without him."

"Ya, but Ma, he was being really odd, I'm telling you. And it's all about this stupid girl. She's not even nice-looking. You know what Michael Gray calls her?"

"I don't need to know. . . ."

"Horsy face. And everybody else—"

"George! What is important here is that Monty likes her. And that's good for Monty. I don't want you giving him a bad time over this. Right now, I

hink Monty could use a little space to sort things
out for himself. Let him reach. Let him stretch.
And I don't think it is such a bad idea for you to
get out and stretch your legs some. So Monty
wants to lie on his bed all afternoon. Well, then
you go hang out with your friends without him.
Don't hover over him, don't waste your Saturday
cleaning the house. . . ."

"Yes, but Ma, this place was really a mess.
There was stuff everywhere. And I have to tell
you, not just Monty's and my stuff. There were
things of yours left in every room in the apartment. You know, there are places for everything.
And I have found that if you can just keep your
things in their places, you will never have to
worry about losing them. Order is a good thing."

Now Ma laughed. I didn't know why, but I was
happy to see it. She reached out and put her hand
on the side of my face. She has very long fingers,
so that when she touches me like that, she can
squeeze my neck muscles with two fingers and rub
my temple with her thumb at the same time. I always remember loving that when I was a kid, and
though I don't like to talk about it much, I don't
hate it now, either.

"George." She laughed softly. "You need to
learn to relax."

I get concerned at times, trying to calculat
how long it's going to be before her fingers don
reach that far anymore.

But that doesn't mean she knows everything
Sometimes even Ma doesn't know what's best fo
Monty like I do.

They make us go to the nine-o'clock mas
every Sunday, the whole school. And we all hav
to sit in assigned rows with our own class. A lot c
people hate it, but I don't think it's the worst wa
to do things. At least it makes things simple, nc
too much thinking for a Sunday morning. It's eve
kind of comfortable, the way you can depend on i
week after week seeing everybody you know sit
ting where he or she belongs, in the same spo
Monty with his class, for example, me with mine
But I did notice this morning that through th
whole service, Monty kept looking over towar
the class right behind mine. He was looking a
her, of course. It got embarrassing for everyone in
volved.

So it was for his own good too, what I did.
only wanted to put things back to where they be
longed.

Monty and I met in the back of the church af
ter mass, like always. Most of the guys didn't han
out—they all just stood around for a few second

said hey, and went on home. We went outside, and there they were, several groups of girls from the fifth, sixth, and seventh grades. They were all standing around on the steps and the sidewalk in their regular groups, talking. All at once the idea came to me, just like a vision, like a religious thing. It was clear what I had to do.

I never intended for him to get hurt at all. All I did was give him some bad advice. Bad advice that I knew was bad advice.

"Okay, Monty, this is going to be your big chance," I told him, pointing at the group Linda O'Leary was in. "Listen, because just this one time, I'm going to give you the can't-miss plan to get your old lady there."

He looked up at me all excited. I had no shame. None. I knew he would listen to me, one, because this girl was making him nuts, and two (and this is the worse part), because deep down he trusts me. I was under a lot of pressure here, and all I wanted to do was put things right.

"All right, do it quickly and do it just the way I say. What you have to do is march down those stairs right now, walk right into Linda's little group, take her by the arm, and without giving her time to think, give her the biggest kiss she ever had."

163

Monty's face froze with his mouth wide open. All his fingers were wiggling nervously by his sides. He bounced from foot to foot and wiggled his head all around, like Mike Tyson at his looniest just before a fight.

"Trust me, Monty. I know her type. She wants a strong guy. You watch—you do it, and she's just going to melt. She'll probably go off someplace with you right now."

He bounced for a second more, like he was waiting for the bell to ring. He made two fists, smacked them against the sides of his legs for courage, and started toward her. After three steps he turned around.

"You don't think maybe I should wait till she's not with all her friends?"

"No way, José," I said. "It'll be ten times more effective when her friends get all jealous."

He nodded hard and shook his fist. As he marched down those big steps, white stone, as wide as the whole church, I noticed how skinny a kid Monty still was. Yet he'd do almost anything. This'll be good, I thought, he'll be back to his old self and that will be best for everyone. Right before he reached Linda's group—he never even slowed down—I wanted to die violently. I wanted the earth to swallow me up, I wanted to go back inside the church and set myself on fire.

Monty was textbook. He walked up behind Linda, and her friends stared at him curiously. He tapped her on the shoulder, and when she turned around, he took her. He grasped her by the elbow, bent her toward him in a sort of dip, and laid one right on her, just like in *Gone with the Wind*. She hadn't even straightened all the way up before she wailed him. I felt it all the way up the stairs. It wasn't even a slap in the face, it was a whole forearm across the side of the head, catching him hardest at the ear. She hit my brother harder than I had ever hit him.

Monty stood there paralyzed while Linda screeched in his face so hard his hair blew back. He had a completely confused look on his face, like he couldn't understand anything anymore. All her friends laughed. Then it spread all around the front of the church like The Wave at a football game, until the kids standing right next to me at the top of the steps were howling. Finally, I saw Monty pull away from her, a huge red mark on the side of his face, while she kept on screaming. He didn't come back up to me. He walked quickly the other way, toward home.

I ran to catch up with him. He wouldn't talk to me. I gave him my five bucks I take every week to buy junk after church. He wouldn't take it. I tried to put it into his hand, but he wouldn't close his fingers around it so it fell to the ground. We left it there. I told him I was sorry. I begged him to hit me. But I was like a ghost to him, and he kept walking quietly.

Suddenly he stopped. I had drifted a few feet behind him, and he wheeled to face me.

"Can't I have anyone?" he said, his voice cracking a little. "I mean, can't I have anyone who's not you? I couldn't have Nat, I couldn't have Chaz . . . couldn't have Fred. I don't have to be you, you know, George. I can be somebody else. I can have another kind of life than what you say."

"Hey," I mumbled. "I wasn't responsible . . ."

Monty stuck a fist up two inches from my nose, shutting me up.

"Did you know, George?" he said to me calmly. "Did you know, when you sent me up there in front of everybody, that something like that was going to happen?"

I sat right there on the curb, staring down into the gutter.

"You did know," Monty said, then walked home.

I sat there. Monty is my responsibility and I hurt him. I was supposed to protect him from guys like me. After a few minutes I got up and ran. Maybe we could step into the ring out back and straighten everything out, get things back to where they were before everything started changing.

When I got to our building, Monty was just hitting the sidewalk. He walked right up to me, in his sweats now.

"I finally see what you mean, about taking care of myself. *By* myself," he said. Then he walked around me and headed down Broadway.

13

Fire in the Hole

Old John from downstairs was on the phone. Everyone else in the rotten building probably would have just let this go on.

"Seen your brother lately?"

"Where is he?"

"He's down in the sewer out front."

"Jee-sus."

"See, the water guys were doin' some work. They went for lunch, left the manhole cover off, the ladder hanging—"

"'Bye, John!"

There was really no reason for me to be surprised. It seemed like every day now Monty was doing something freaky. Disappearing for long stretches, spending hours with books like *Your Pectorals Are Your Friends*, while his homework went undone, coming home covered in soot one day, with scuffs and bumps many other days. Still, when I got outside and saw a half dozen people staring into the ground to watch "The Monty Show," I almost wanted to pretend he wasn't mine.

"Monty," I yelled.

His voice came back up like an echo in a valley. "Everybody back! I think she's gonna blow!"

The whole crowd laughed. Two old guys from our building, both named Johnson, elbowed each other. They have nothing to do all day but listen to police-band radio, and are the first ones on the street when a tire screeches.

"Monty, this is George."

"We're gonna take her down, captain," he answered.

I got madder every time he got a laugh. An older kid, smoking a cigarette, flicked a lit match down into the sewer.

"Fire in the hole," Monty called. "Fire in the hole."

Johnson and Johnson were wheezing from laughter. I pointed at the kid with the smokes, directly across the manhole from me. "You do that again, junior, and you're goin' in the hole after it." Nobody laughed, and the kid just waved me off, which was a relief because he looked like he could bury me.

"Get up out of there," I said.

"Women and children first," he called. "Don't worry about me, just save yourselves."

The only thing left to do was go in after him myself. As I walked to where the ladder was hooked, I got a tap on the shoulder.

"And what do you think you're doing?" said the sewer worker with the yellow hard hat and boots. There was another just like him behind him, sipping coffee. I opened my mouth to answer, but Monty interrupted.

"Ramming speed. We're gonna take her out, boys."

"What the f—" The workers brushed me aside and looked down into the hole.

"That's his brother, that's Mental Monty," one of the three little kids said as they ran away. The men looked at me and I just shrugged. The wise-guy kid shuffled away. One of the Johnsons had one of those canes that unfolds into a chair, and was parked on it.

"Hey kid," the sewer man yelled. "Get the hell out of there."

"Uh-oh. Iceberg ho!" Monty said.

One of the workers, the one with the coffee, laughed. The other did not, and said, "All right then, I'm coming down after you." And into the hole he went. He was pretty steamed, and was down and back in less than a minute. He must have climbed right over Monty, because when they came up, Monty was in front.

"You're lucky I don't have you arrested," the mad one said. He didn't even come all the way out of the sewer before going back down. The other one leaned over to Monty. "I was seven the first time I went down. It's a thrill you never get over."

I grabbed Monty by the arm and led him toward the apartment. Johnson and Johnson stayed to watch the work.

"What's the matter with you?" I said, and as I turned him to face me, I saw Monty had a good, puffy fat lip. "What happened to your mouth?"

He pulled his arm out of my grip. "I must have bumped it on the ladder."

"What did you go down there for?"

"You know how it is. Sometimes a guy just has to get away."

"Away? In the sewer, Monty?"

"It's not so bad, you know. It's this giant brick tube. It's a lot like being inside the smokestack over at the brake-pad factory."

I almost couldn't hear his words as I tried to figure out what was going on with him, and where he *really* got the fat lip. When I noticed his high tops were squishing, realized he'd been dangling his feet in that water, I stopped and stared at his feet. He kept walking.

"Wait a minute," I yelled, shaking my head. "You've been *inside the smokestack at the brake-pad factory?*" The brake-pad factory. Next door to Archie's.

He broke into a trot and headed squishing down the block. He was doing a lot of running these days too. Told Ma he was interested in maybe joining the junior high track team next year, which she seemed pretty thrilled about at first because track sure wasn't "Satan's sport," as she called boxing. But she never actually *saw* him run. Your basic skinny track geek doesn't bob and jab while he runs.

But this couldn't last. The bumps and the general oddness were starting to show, and Ma was starting to see it. She was seeing Dad. Dad with the heart of a lion and the head of a starfish. She was, like Archie said, left hurtin' when the Big Man fell. Since then she saw Dad in a lot of things—a curled fist, a cut that wouldn't clot, and everything having anything to do with the human skull. And though she was trying hard not to, she was seeing Dad in Monty. And there, I think she was seeing pretty good.

14

Adam's Apple

When I walked into the living room, Monty was watching a music video in which Michael Jackson was screaming at the sky, smashing windshields, slapping himself hard in the crotch, and turning into a panther. It was eight o'clock in the morning.

"Mr. Rogers has a new hairstyle, huh?" I said as I sat down next to him. He inched away from me.

"Ma said to eat the hard-boiled eggs that are in the pot." He didn't take his eyes off the TV when he talked. "There should be plenty. She cooked every egg in the house so I couldn't drink 'em."

Monty held a tall glass of something that looked like chocolate milk. I reached over to get it, and in his daze he just gave it up. "This tastes like sand, man," I said, and stuck it back into his still-curled hand. He tipped the glass and drank it all down.

"Ahhh."

"Monty, what is that? You got some intestinal trouble or something?"

"It's my powdered protein drink."

"Your powdered *what*?"

"Protein. Three or four glasses of that a day, and it's gonna turn me into the Hulkster." He finally turned to look at me, leaning way over into my face and leering. "And I wouldn't want to be *you* when that happens."

"Are you for real? You're in *space*, monkey-boy."

He kept smiling at me, then pointed toward the back door with his thumb. Meaning the backyard. Meaning the ring. "Got three minutes to spare before we leave for school?"

I didn't want to encourage the mania that had a grip on him, but if there was ever a time he could use a lesson, this was it.

"Let's rock," I said.

He aimed the remote like a gun and snapped off the TV. I followed him out of the room and down the stairs. He was limping.

"What's the matter with your leg?" I said.

"My hip hurts. But I don't care."

"Monty, twelve-year-olds don't get sore hips."

"What can I tell you? I'm ahead of my time."

In the ring he kept smiling at me, which was

174

kind of irritating and not very smart. His hands were down at his sides and he was standing still.

Pop. Pop. I threw one medium hook to either side of his head. "Lesson three *and* lesson four, Monty. Don't stop moving for any reason. And keep your hands up and your mouth closed, or you're gonna swallow teeth."

He laughed at me. He knew these things. He *never* drops his hands. He was actually enjoying getting hit.

I kept circling, stalking him, then stepping up to strike. I hit him fifteen or twenty times without taking anything back. All he would do was tip his head down so that I was ringing shots off the very top of his skull. Then he'd look up and smile again. His point appeared to be to show me how tough he was. It was sort of working: My hands were starting to ache.

"What do I do?" I started muttering to myself. I riffled through my own lessons. Lesson one? Lesson five, lesson six, lesson seven, lesson ten. Dope. Lesson two!

I stepped close and faked a head shot. He tipped his head down. One two three four five six seven eight straight uncontested body blows, and the new Mighty Monty was down.

When I lifted him up, he was a little green.

"What are you, a rookie?" I scolded him. "I went easy on you. You take that attitude of yours up to somebody who maybe doesn't like you so much, and you ain't coming home that night."

He pulled away from me and started walking, a little hunched over, to school. I walked behind him.

"I'm embarrassed, Monty. I put in a lot of hours making sure you knew how to take care of yourself, and you come out here fighting like . . . like a football player. I'm trying to give you everything I know. But I feel like I'm failing. What's happening to your skills? What's happening to your head?"

"Shut up, George."

"What, are you gonna get tough with me now, Monty?"

He stopped in the middle of the sidewalk and turned around to face me. "If I have to, yes."

"You'll excuse me if I don't find that too frightening, after the show you just put on."

He took his finger and poked me in the chest. He tapped, not hard, but just enough for me to know he was there. "You might bang me up, George, but I'll tell you this: You ain't gonna *enjoy* fighting me. Nobody ever *likes* fighting me." Where had I heard that before?

He turned around and started marching before

I could say anything. For once I didn't challenge him for the last word. I just walked slowly on behind him. At a distance. I gave him first ten, then thirty feet of lead. Watching him limp solemnly down the street, I wondered what was going on.

"Monty," I yelled when he reached the gate at the entrance to the school yard. He stopped dead, to let me know he heard, but didn't turn around. "We have to have a talk. Meet me right there, at the gate, after school."

He hesitated, then walked to the building.

About an hour before the school day ended, Sister Rita called me up to her desk. "George, I'm going to send you home a little early. . . ."

I bolted toward the door.

"George, come here. I just got a message that Monty was sent home sick a little while ago. We know that there is no one at home to look after him at this hour, so we decided it would be best for you to go take care of things—you know, the way you do."

The little scam artist, I thought as I left the school yard. Although he did manage to get *both* of us out a little early. Still, he can't be pulling this stuff.

Or had I hurt him? He really *didn't* look too

good last I saw. A hard shot in the gut can really do a guy some damage—nobody knows that better than me. I got all hot in the face thinking about it then broke into a trot for the rest of the way.

When I got to the apartment, it was empty. Monty's navy-blue pants, light-blue shirt, and navy clip-on were balled on his bed.

I went back to "That little scam artist." I was still shaking my head and choreographing what I was going to do to him (figure-four leglock with full scream) when I opened up the closet to hang up my clothes and his. It practically jumped out at me, that big can of protein powder on the shelf. He forgot to stash it behind the guitar. There was a picture of a white-blond guy on the label who looked like the Michelin tire guy with a thirty-inch waist.

I reached up and grabbed the can to check it out. Something fell off the top of it. I recognized it the second it passed by my face, before I even lowered my eyes to the floor where it landed. A white piece of plastic in the shape of a semicircle. With bite marks all over it. It was a fighter's mouthpiece.

I stood for a few seconds staring at the thing in my palm, then at the Michelin man in my other hand. I threw the can on the closet floor, grabbed my jacket, and ran out the door, to Archie's, squeezing the mouthpiece in my fist.

"Archie," I screamed from the big doorway. Guys were throwing leather in two different rings, making some pretty savage noise, but for a second they stopped.

"Georgie," Archie called. He motioned the fighters to get back into it, then came over. He was smiling, but he was a little twitchy.

"How's it hangin', George? I didn't know if I'd see you back here."

"Ya, well I hear you got a hot new fighter in the stable that maybe I oughta see."

Archie put both of his stony old hands up in front of his face, like I was going to go at him. "I don't let nobody hurt him, George, I promise."

"You *know* that's not the problem, Archie. You *know* what's wrong with this." I had to yell at him, partly to be heard over the fighting, the drum rolls of punches, partly because Archie was playing the dunce with me. "Where is he? I'm taking him outta here."

I walked around Archie to go looking for Monty. From behind, Archie grabbed my shoulders. "Wait now, George." Without looking, I threw an elbow as hard as I could into his stomach. That belly was kind of big, and round, but it was as hard as a truck tire. I don't think I bothered him at all. "Sit down, George. I want you to hear me out." Archie grabbed two round wooden stools, the kind the boxers sit on between rounds. We were even closer to the action now, where the guys in the ring were throwing for real. Every punch sounded like a baseball bat hitting a door.

Archie got very close. "George, you're right. This ain't the place for your brother. Your ma sure don't want him in here. You don't want him in here. And much as I truly love having him—having both of you as a matter of fact—around, I don't want him in here. This game is my life, but I know it's just for them that ain't got nothin' else. But the problem is, our boy got the bug. Trust me on this, Monty's got it bad. I seen it in a thousand kids before. I seen it in your dad. And you can't kill the bug by yanking him outta here. It's kinda like a tick: You just leave the head under the skin, then it grows back."

"Ya, Archie, well if my mother finds out about this, she's gonna yank the heads off of all three of us."

Archie laughed, sat back on his stool. "I remember your ma's fire, boy, and I have no interest in sparkin' it."

"So then what are you talking about?"

"I'm talkin' 'bout let me fix it. I can work it out of his system. This ain't no pretty life to begin with, George, you know that. And there is some hard shit to swallow that a good handler don't show to a young pup until much later on, if he don't want the pup to quit. I just suggest I accelerate Monty's program."

Monty came walking out of the locker room at the far end of the gym. He dropped a mop into a bucket by the door, went to the free-weight area, and began stacking steel plates on the rack.

"See that?" Archie said. "The kid never stops. He's a horse. But I've already started the plan by *workin'* his ass to death."

I stood. Archie stayed on his stool. I watched Monty heaving weights floor to rack, floor to rack, like a man on a chain gang. His limp was gone, unless he was just hiding it from his athlete friends. He seemed awfully strong all of a sudden. Two long lean fighters, carrying gym bags, passed Monty on their way into the locker room. The first, a kid really, rubbed Monty's head and went on by. The second, a foot taller than my brother and maybe forty pounds heavier—a junior middleweight I'd say—dropped his bag. He and Monty immediately went into a dance of fakes, shuffles, feints, and pulled punches. Monty looked smooth as a snake.

"I don't know about this, Archie," I said, still looking off at Monty.

My uncle, still squatting on that little round

stool, tugged my hand. I looked down at him. He looked sad, he looked beat.

"God, you look so much like your dad," he said to me.

Lesson one: Focus. I had to look away or I couldn't think straight. I looked back at Monty, to see Monty looking back at me. Slowly he started walking over as Archie talked more quickly.

"Please, George, you gotta let me do this. You gotta give me the chance here to do everybody a favor, 'specially your ma. I can't give her Tommy back, but I can at least give her back this little one. And then, who knows. . . ."

When Monty reached us, he stood beside Archie, who stood up and put his arm around him. "That's right, George," Archie announced, "this boy's startin' to look like a real pugilist. And there ain't nobody can handle him but his uncle Archibald."

Archie nodded at me and winked. Monty stared at me anxiously. "We're outta here, right?" Monty said.

"Right," I said.

Archie put an arm around each of us as he saw us out. Nobody said anything until we were almost out the door and Archie whispered in my ear, "Please?"

182

"You gonna make me stop, George?" Monty said as we walked beneath the tracks.

I didn't answer right away, and he didn't push it. A block later, I said, "What do you want to be when you grow up, Monty?"

He thought this was changing the subject, so he loosened up.

"Bigger than you." He laughed.

I stopped walking, hopped up on the hood of a parked car, and sat. "Get over here." I called him with two fingers, then patted the hood beside me. He hopped up. "Monty," I said, "what do you want to be when you grow up?"

"For real?"

"Really real."

"I want to be a guitar player and a boxer. Then I want to be president."

"I'm not screwing around here."

"Neither am I. I can play guitar and fight, both. And the oldest rock 'n' rollers and fighters are still younger than the youngest presidents, so I'd have the time to do it all."

He was staring at me so seriously, like he was already running for office.

"Okay, Monty, but if it turns out you can only do one thing, what would you do?"

Monty slid down off the car and stood squarely

in front of me. He held his fists up alongside his shoulders and said, almost like he was apologizing, "Look at me, George. You know I'm a fighter."

That wasn't really news, but still it shook me up to hear it. As he stood there posed like a bare-knuckle fighter from a hundred years ago, I took his advice and looked at him. He was bigger. I didn't know if it was bigger than yesterday or bigger than last month, but he had put on some bulk that I hadn't noticed before. He was still only up to my nose, but his shoulders were as wide as mine. His hands and feet were big too, like he was a puppy that was still growing into them. I knew right there that Monty was going to wind up a cruiserweight at least, probably a heavyweight like our father. I'd never be better than a middleweight. And sprouting out from above his collar was this brand-new nub of an Adam's apple.

Monty knew the score. Nobody had lectured him, but he knew his answer wasn't going to thrill anybody. He lowered his hands to his sides. "You gonna try to make me stop, George?"

I got off the car and nudged him to walk on. "Nope," I said. His mouth dropped open in shock, and that's how it hung as he stared at me all the way home.

When we walked in the house, Ma was sitting

in her reading chair in the living room. At first we didn't notice her as we walked down the hall.

"Hey guys," she called. We backed up and went in. Monty kissed her quickly, then disappeared into the bedroom, leaving me standing in front of her. She could smell something.

"George," she said. "What is going on with your brother? He's acting very, very peculiar."

I tried to walk out of the room while I answered her, to be casual. "You know how it is, Ma."

"Excuse me, sir, would you come back in here a minute?" I did. "No, George, I don't know how it is, that's why I'm asking. Is there something you're not telling me?"

"He's okay. It's just, you know what I think it is, it's that he's just getting his Adam's apple. It's making him weird." I put my hand on her shoulder. "Remember when I got mine? I sure was hell, wasn't I?"

Usually a little trip down memory lane like that was just the ticket for Ma. She likes that memory lane stuff. But this time I got nothing. She just sat there, all distracted, until she looked hard into me. "Sit down, George," she said quietly, and pointed at the sofa across from her. We sat for an uncomfortable minute or so while she took on that distant, distracted look again.

"Your dad liked to tell me," she finally said, "about how his parents tried to keep him out of the ring. About the brawls he would have with his father over it. It was the reason he left home at sixteen and got himself into the army. That's where he started fighting seriously, and he never stopped. He often said that that business with his parents made him a more determined fighter, and ultimately made a man out of him." Suddenly Ma looked at me and smiled. Then she quickly looked away again, to wherever it was she was looking. "When I met your dad, I was seventeen years old and had never heard a more romantic story in my life. Over the years, I heard him tell it to other people every once in a while, and it still sounded . . . oh, heroic."

"It is a great story, Ma." It made me sad as hell. I knew the story. She knew I knew the story. She knew why I knew the story. And she was going to tell me anyway, because she needed me to be sad with her.

"Then, in the last year of his life, your father told me that story every day. I don't mean he told me the story a lot. I mean every . . . single . . . day, as if I'd never heard it. Almost as if *he'd* never heard it." She closed her eyes and sort of sank into her chair. "Georgie, the story was not romantic or heroic anymore."

I closed my eyes too. If I hadn't closed them right then, I couldn't have talked. "He could have quit," I said.

"He couldn't," she said. "He was simply incapable. Every day there would be a couple of periods—around breakfast time and again before dinner—when he was clear in his thoughts. We would talk about it. So many times, he was quitting. He would give me his great big teddy-bear hugs and talk about spending more time with you boys, training kids with his brother. It was such a wonderful picture, I got excited every time he said it. But he'd get up the next day, kiss me in the morning, kiss me in the evening, and fight all in between. Couldn't even remember saying it. There's a time, George, early on, when a fighter has the power to walk away. But that time passes quickly, and then . . ."

She just stopped talking, and we sat there in the dark, because we had our eyes closed still. I opened mine to look at her. She wasn't just closing her eyes, but squeezing them tight, like praying. It was then I knew she knew it all. Everything. There isn't a person on the earth who hates boxing more than my mother does, but now that I think about it, there probably isn't anyone who knows more about it. At least about fighters. And she was saying the same thing Archie was saying: If we yank Monty out, like Dad's parents tried, we're cooked.

I walked over to her, put my hand on her shoulder. She opened her eyes and looked up at me.

"Trust me, Ma, I won't let it happen. I'll swallow him whole first."

Footsteps in the Dark

It was a long time later that they shared this story with me. It was a shock to find that Ma had done what she swore she'd never do, which was to step into a gym again. But I knew it was the truth because almost down to the exact same words, Archie and Ma came and told me the story about the one and only time they got near each other since my dad died.

When he first heard her voice, Archie's head was thrown all the way back, a stream of Gatorade shooting into his mouth from one of the plastic squeeze bottles he always carried. Six thirty A.M. and he'd already broken his first sweat.

"This new place reeks, just like the old place, Archie," she said, her voice like a gunshot in that early-morning silence.

He was standing in front of a mirror in the free-weight area, as far as you could get from the front door. And though he hadn't spoken to her in years, he knew immediately who it was.

"Smells like warm Gatorade, don'tcha think?" he said as he mopped his face with a yellow towel.

"Smells like sweat," she said. As she walked across the gym toward him, the sound of her heels clacking on the bare hardwood told him how close she was. "And it smells like a public bathroom, and it smells like liniment, and it smells like very young blood."

When she was six feet away, Archie turned to look at her. She stopped. He smiled at her, slowly, kind of unsure, like a face on Mount Rushmore trying to smile. "That's what I said. Warm Gatorade. All them things are in Gatorade."

She wouldn't smile for him. She stared into him, no shying, no blinking, no looking at his tattoo or his belly. All eye. She can kill a guy with that if she wants.

"You remembered," Archie said. "You remembered how early I open up, and the way we—I—always liked to get in that first workout in the dark."

"Remembered?" she shot, angry at the word. She marched forward, toward Archie, then right

190

past him, to the hundreds of fight posters on the office wall. As she spoke, she stared at them, following them up and down like a war memorial. "Remembered, Archie? You're surprised I *remembered*? Could it be possible that you don't know I remember it all? Every *day*, I remember it. I live with it. Every glove thrown in every minute of every round of every fight I remember, damn you." She pointed to a poster advertising a ten-fight card on Thanksgiving 1977. "Remember that one, Archie? That was a big win for our boy, wasn't it? A mere three-day hospital stay. I guess we were all lucky that guy Cooney didn't have anything more than a terrific left-hand lead, huh? If he were a two-handed fighter, maybe George wouldn't have ever been born."

Archie couldn't speak. He just watched her back as she faced the wall. She ran her hand up and down, side to side as she paced Archie's "Wall of Honor." Every three or four posters she would stop and slap her hand hard on a picture of Dad's hammered face, or just his name way down low on the list of warm-up fighters.

"Of course I remember. I always did remember it and always will, without any help from you. So maybe you can imagine how I've felt lately when I've been awakened by a ghost, by the footsteps in the dark around five A.M."

Though she couldn't see him, Archie covered his face with his hands. Hiding. Covering up the only way he knew.

"You know what I first thought, Archie?" she said. "The first couple of times I heard that stirring before dawn, I thought, in my grogginess, that all was well. I let myself think that that was my Tommy, cracking eggs into a glass, stretching out his quadriceps over the back of my kitchen chair. So I lay back and I smiled, thinking my life was still whole.

"Funny, huh? Until, of course, I snapped out of it and realized that this quiet nightmare pulling me out of sleep—all over again—was all too real, and this time even worse."

Then she fell forward, pressing both hands flat against the wall and letting her head drop. Archie heard her deep breaths, all loaded full of voice, and hurried to her. Cautiously he put his hands over her shoulders.

She spun, shook out of his grasp, and slapped his face hard.

"You can't have him," she yelled.

When he said nothing, she slapped him again, harder, reddening her own hand. Archie again stood like a statue, as he would have done if she'd hit him a thousand more times.

"Do you understand me, Archie? You *cannot* have him. I will not watch this again. By the time Tom died, it was almost a relief, after what his life had become the last few years. I won't let it happen to Monty. I'd just as soon see him in a box as see him in a ring."

Archie waited for her to spend it all before he tried to answer. He knew he couldn't tell her what she wanted to hear.

"There's nothing you can do about it. You try to stop him and it'll just get worse."

"You think *I* don't know that better than anyone who ever lived? Who do you think you're talking to here, Archie? I know I can't stop it— that's the only reason I haven't got him chained to a radiator in his bedroom already. But *you*." She jammed a jagged, bitten fingernail into his chest. "You have the power."

Archie shook his head sadly, backing away from her like a scared animal.

"You know I can't. Now, we been down this road before, you and me. I still got the deepest scars to prove it. If the boy's a fighter, he's a fighter. And if he is, it's best that I'm there to look out for him."

She narrowed her eyes and started growling

words. "Yes, and we all know how well—"

Archie jumped forward, holding out his hand like a stop signal, the hand as big as her face.

"I won't let you say that," he said in his slow, deep voice, somehow a whisper and somehow bigger than his regular voice. "You can say whatever other hurtful thing you need to, to make yourself feel better, but don't say another thing 'bout how I cared for my brother."

They held that position for several seconds, each holding ground, and each giving in some.

"Well," she finally said, softer now, "I just don't believe that anymore. Archie, I believe you can do something about this. And I believe you are the *only* one who can. I'm not going to say a word about it to Monty, because I am afraid of driving him further into it. But there is no way this is going to happen."

She paused, then pointed aggressively in Archie's direction again, simply adding, "You . . ."

Archie was in her path as she headed back to the exit. She walked directly toward him, then stopped a foot away from him.

"I hope I don't ever have to see you again, Archie," she said. But it wasn't with anger this time.

"I hope not neither," he said, the same way, smiling.

It seemed for a second like they were going to touch each other, hug, pat shoulders or something. But they didn't. Couldn't get any closer, like a couple of magnets repelling each other, or like there was somebody standing between them.

Archie silently turned and went back to lifting weights. Ma tracked back across the big empty gym and out the door.

A Boy's Best Friend

It was still dark out when I got up to deliver my papers. Then I jogged through the whole route. When I finished, I went straight to Archie's. I was sitting on his stoop when he got there to open up.

"You're not getting it done, Archie," I told him.

"I know it," he said. "Come inside."

We walked upstairs and Archie flipped on the big overhead lights. He threw his nylon bag and his old navy pea coat right there on the floor. I dropped my canvas newspaper bag.

"There's some stuff I never figured on, George. He's a tough kid, our Monty. I suspect you can thank yourself for that." He ambled over to the heavy bags to start his own workout. I followed, held the bag for him. "One thing complicating the matter is that, well, Monty's good." Archie hit the bag a few times, pitty-pat stuff. "It's a lot harder to kill the bug when the boy is good at the game."

"Come on, Arch. I just laid a whippin' on him yesterday. How good could he be?"

"Like he was born to it." Archie slammed a stiff left into the bag, knocking my jaw out of position. Then he peered around the bag smiling big at me. "Be fair, now. Don't measure him by you. We both know that, like it or no, you was born to it too. And you was born to it *first*. But George, that brother of yours is takin' on kids, mean mothers, thirteen years old, and *handling* them. Boys big as you, boys I been schoolin' for two years. I'll tell ya, he's good enough that I wish he wasn't my nephew, I wish he was just some dumb ol' hungry street animal. I could take him a long way."

I stepped away from the bag when Archie attacked it, throwing three-punch hook combinations followed by a scary uppercut. His feet stayed flat when he hit, and you could feel it through the floor.

"Archie, it's been two weeks. You said . . ."

"And that ain't even the kicker. I'd have had him out of here by now anyway 'cept that the roots, the roots of this fascination are runnin' deep. A lot deeper than I figured." Archie motioned me toward one of the two full-size rings in the gym. "You want to shadow? C'mon, it's good exercise and it ain't strictly fightin'."

I hesitated, then climbed in the ring after him. He had on a pair of the thin workout gloves that are made for hitting the bag. He handed me a pair.

"All right, tell me about the roots."

"I tell you, there ain't no quit in the boy. None whatsoever," he said, dodging, shuffling his feet, faking punches that stopped an inch short of my nose. I danced in a circle around him. "Seems he's been taking care of some business, y'know, taking it out on the street. . . ."

"Ya, he has."

"And, well, he seems to think that there ain't no place to go but up. Like he's settling all his scores, righting every wrong, and now he's anglin' for new challenges. It is a very intoxicating thing, y'know, George, when a young man first throws that big hand and watches all his problems just drop at his feet."

I hit Archie twice in the breadbasket, then started circling again.

"Atta boy," he said. He looked proud. My heart started pumping hard. "So the crazy part is . . ."

I raced back in and threw a flurry, even landing a light one on Archie's chin. My feet were flying as I got back on my bicycle and stalked, jabbing, jabbing.

"You boys do my heart more good than any-body I worked with in ten years. The way you take the body, nobody wants to do that anymore." Archie wore an enormous grin on his face as he lumbered after me. I kept moving. Whenever he would cut me off and get close, Archie would fire those old fists past my head on both sides. I got so pumped I forgot that he was missing on purpose.

I lunged forward one more time when Archie again had his mouth open to tell me what I came to find out. I hit him a sharp one on his nose, right on the button, and it trickled blood instantly. We both stopped moving. Archie wasn't mad, but he wasn't grinning at me anymore either. But then he was again. He laughed and stuck out a jab at about a hundredth of the power he'd hit the bag with, and I was on my back looking into the lights.

"I'm sorry, Georgie," he said as he picked me up and sat me on a stool. "You must not have been ready for that one."

"It's okay," I wheezed. "You just knocked the wind out of me."

Archie punched himself hard in the forehead. "Big . . . stupid . . . lummox," he said, giving him-self a rap with every word.

"Really," I said. "I'm fine. Don't hit yourself like that."

"What're you kidding me? My head is rock and my hands are glass. If I could only throw a punch hard enough to hurt myself, I'd be heavyweight champ today."

We both laughed, and Archie patted my cheek. "I only wish you could come here and beat me up every day. . . . But anyway, Monty."

"Ya, Monty," I said.

"He asks me a lot of questions. About your old man. About all kinds of other fighters. Then one day he asks me this strange question. He wants to know if any of the guys who fought your father were still around. And if they had any boys who was fighters."

"Oh no."

"Oh ya. And the thing is, sure, some of them use this very gym. George, Monty's got this idea that somehow he's fighting along with his old man. That somehow your dad is here, is his friend, is his fighting buddy. Sometimes he'll be off in a corner all in his own world, or fightin' in the mirror, and he'll be talkin'. And I know who he's talkin' to, I've heard him. It's become his focus, and George, I don't mind telling you it's spooking me a little. I try to tell him, Monty, you can't mess with what's past, this here life is *yours* alone, not your father's. But I don't see that I'm gettin' through."

"Exactly how many times has he been punched in the head here, Arch? You do have him wearing headgear, don't you?"

"Georgie, don't scoff. He ain't the first boy to feel the pull. It ain't that unusual, 'specially in this business, 'specially when he has this kinda dream picture of his father."

Archie turned away from me and walked to the far side of the ring. He rested his hands on the top rope.

Still on my stool, I talked at his back. "So Archie. Tell him how it really was, can't you? Tell him the real stuff about what happened to Dad. I mean, you were there, he'll listen to you."

"Ya," he said quietly. "My most favorite song—well the only song I ever remember liking anyway—has a line in it that goes, 'Still, a man hears what he wants to hear And disregards the rest.' George, my boy, that's a specially smart song because the name of that song is 'The Boxer.' They got it right."

He was frustrating me, I guess because I had expected him to just solve everything. "So? Is that it? Did you shoot your shot and now he's just gonna get punched in the damn head for the rest of his life, and wind up . . ."

I didn't mean to start that, and I never would

have finished if Archie didn't pick it up. "Like your father," he said.

"Or like you," I shouted.

It was a big empty hall, and with nobody but Archie and me there I heard my words bounce back to me again, and again. Though my stomach was still fluttery, I got right off my stool and went over to him. Before I could apologize, he spoke.

"Like me. You're right, boy. *That* would be even worse."

I pulled his arm to turn him toward me. Not that I could move him if he didn't want to be moved. "Don't listen to me, Arch. You must've scrambled my brains with that TKO."

He stared down into me. His nose was still bleeding. Those old wounds weep for hours. "George, don't worry. You ain't tellin' me nothin' about myself I don't already know. I'm just glad you turned out smart, that you know better. An' we're gonna make that crazy Monty understand what you already know. He's comin' back here first of next week, right after school. I'll take care of it then, and he won't be back here no more."

"How are you gonna do that?"

"You wanna know that, you're welcome to be here. Fact, maybe it's a good idea you do come by. So you come, you see, you don't, you don't. 'Cause

I got a feelin' Monty ain't gonna talk about it afterward."

He followed me to the door, where I picked up my newspaper bag. "Gotta get to school," I told him.

"Yes, you do," he said. Then, after a pause, "I'm gonna miss him, George."

I wished I could help him with that, but I had no choice. I was confused lately, but I knew one thing: I had a job given to me a long time ago, and if Monty became a fighter, then I had failed.

"Ya," I said as I looked down at the sidewalk.

As I walked out, he followed me down a few steps to tell me, "I had a really good time. You know, this mornin'."

I stopped at the bottom of the stairs and looked up at his slanted, dopey smile. I rubbed my breadbasket. "I did too, Archie."

17
Let It Bleed

I was uncommonly happy to see Monday roll around. Monty and I walked to school together without saying too much. His head was in the gym already. So was mine. After school, I gave him a long lead as he headed in the direction of Archie's, and I followed.

By the time I'd walked up the stairs, Monty was already in the ring with somebody. Archie was leaning over the rope watching. The two of them, Monty and the kid, who was a head taller than him, were moving like gears around each other. One would jab, the other would block. One would try to lead with a straight right—a dumb thing to do—and the other would duck under it. They both had nearly perfect footwork, no crossover steps, no flatfootedness, get in, stick, get out.

It was almost beautiful, the way these two kids flowed and wore on each other. I found myself staring. Archie said nothing but the occasional "Mmmm," or "Right," which meant that they were doing it right. Then the big kid let one hang. To most people what he did wouldn't really stick out, but we all knew boxing, and to Archie, Monty, and me, well, the kid might as well have thrown off all his clothes. He threw this lazy jab, no bad intentions behind it at all, as if he were just killing time. But worse, he let it hang there after Monty ducked it, instead of yanking it back the way he should. Like he was shot out of a cannon, Monty did exactly what he was supposed to do, slamming an overhand right straight over that hanging jab, catching the kid flush on the temple. I found myself miming the same punch, and watching Archie do it too. That's how natural it was.

The kid bounced when he hit the canvas. Then he rolled backward. Archie went right in to see to him, while Monty stood bouncing on the balls of his feet. The kid sat up, shaking his head-gear back and forth, his mouth wide open as Archie pulled out his mouthpiece.

"That's it for now, boys," Archie said loudly when he saw that the kid was fine. Then he got right in the kid's face, while he was still sitting. "Don't you *ever* leave that fucking hand hanging there like that. You hear me? You ever leave a tater like that hanging there again, I'll climb in there and knock your ass out myself. You wanna get killed? You wanna be dead?"

It was a little embarrassing to watch, but Archie meant it. I knew he wasn't just trying to motivate the kid because his face was so blue and the green veins in his neck were bulging. He took it personally.

When Archie turned to leave the ring, he walked past Monty, who had the faintest grin on his face, shining through the black headgear. "Forget about it," Archie barked, slapping the leather padding over Monty's forehead. "It's over. You dwell on something like that and you wind up right where *he* is. Take off the gear—I got something to show you."

Monty stripped off the gloves and helmet, then trailed after Archie to the office. "We're going to the film room," Archie said. He opened the door, framed by that huge wall of fight posters, ushered Monty in first, then turned and waved me over. I didn't think he even saw me. I know Monty didn't.

When I slipped in the door, it was dark except for the flickering TV light. The office was set up like a mini movie theater, with gray metal folding chairs facing a big-screen TV with a VCR on a tall rolling stand like the schools use. Monty looked over his shoulder at me. I couldn't make out his expression, but he just turned away again as Archie cued up the tape.

"This was back when ESPN was just starting out," he said as we looked at a long shot of a nearly empty fight arena. "Back in seventy-nine. They would put just about anything on the air they could get their hands on." Monty and Arch sat side by side right in front of the set as the camera closed in on the two men receiving their instructions at center ring. One of the fighters—heavyweights—was from Philadelphia, a short, thick guy with slabs of muscle covering his whole body. The other was taller, thinner, with wide pink worms of scar tissue above and below each eye and on his top lip. Monty sat quietly, attentively. He knew Archie showed films regularly, to illustrate various technical points of the game, so he didn't think much of it. He didn't realize right off who the man with the scars was. I knew immediately it was Dad.

They weren't ten seconds into the fighting before Archie chuckled, proud, saying, "He sure was a devil at the body, your old man."

A second or so passed, then it kicked in.

Monty whipped his face toward Archie, who didn't look back. Then he looked back at me. None of us spoke. Monty turned to watch.

It was unbelievable, the bad intentions in that ring. Dad threw leather, from the heels every time. The granite man from Philadelphia threw back, two for one. The broadcaster was *yelling* the blow by blow, not a minute into the bout. "NO defense!" he screamed. "These two warriors are here for only one reason—to take the other man out—and soon."

He was right. They were both going for the early knockout. Dad hammered away at the body. The other guy was headhunting. They just leaned on each other and punched without moving their feet until the Philly guy pushed Dad, who backpedaled to the ropes. Precisely at the moment that Dad bounced off the ropes, the guy threw himself at him with a straight right hand. Dad tried to block this one but it made no difference—the big fist just exploded between the gloves and smashed square into Dad's face. The blood started running from his nose.

It didn't seem to bother Dad much. He just tried to go on fighting from the ropes. I saw Monty straighten up in his chair. Archie was a statue.

Again the Philly guy threw Dad like a doll off

the ropes, and again he blasted a straight right off his head. Dad's knees buckled, but he straightened. A cut opened wide over his right eye. Archie shook his big head and put his arm around Monty. "He was always a bleeder, the poor kid," Archie said. "There's nothing you can do about it. No way to prepare for it, no way to stop it."

"Oh my," the announcer screamed. "That eye is a mess. It's gone from pulp to hamburger in seconds!" The fighters locked in a clinch, and when the referee broke it up, the other man's head smashed into Dad's lip, splitting it wide open. The small crowd said "ooohh" all at once, like a record playing backward. Archie pointed the remote control and turned off the sound as Monty nuzzled deeper under his big arm.

For the next few minutes I couldn't feel anything. My hands, my feet, my self, seemed not to be there as the fight went on in silence. The whole thing sort of floated there before us. Through the end of round one, the closeups of Archie and the cut man working on Dad between rounds, and into round two.

It was clear by that second round that Dad was fighting a man who was much stronger. As it wore on, Dad's punches did less and less, bouncing off the other guy's gloves, or his face, or his belly, all with the same no effect. The other guy, though, seemed to feed on it. He got stronger, faster, younger as he tore into my father, making him grab his side one time, making him press his gloves to his own face to protect those eyes.

"Philly fighters," Archie said. "They're pit bulls. But so was your old man. Neither one of these guys had the goddamn sense to take a step backward."

By the end of the second round the man from Philadelphia was throwing his big left hand at will, hitting my father every time right in the eye. The eye that was shut so tight that Dad had to turn his head unnaturally to try to watch his right side with his left eye. Monty was hunched over, his body jerking with spasms as Archie held him tight. He looked little, nothing like the big-shouldered kid I'd recently noticed or the smooth boxer who had just dropped somebody ten minutes earlier.

And I still felt nothing. I just stared as the camera pulled close on Archie and Dad between the second and third rounds. "Never shoulda been a third," Archie said sadly. The cut man put a piece of ice on Dad's lip, which was tearing and tearing like a wet paper towel. Archie slapped the ice away and started screaming in the cut man's face. As if he knew what I was thinking, Archie answered, "We had to let the lip bleed. It's the eye cuts, the blood running into the eyes that kill a guy." With one hand the cut man pressed a piece of frozen metal on the puffy eye to reduce the swelling. With the thumb of the other hand, he worked a mixture that was like cement right into the wide cut over the eye bones. "They have to carve that shit out with a knife later," Archie said. Every five seconds or so, my father would lean over and spit a bucket of blood. During the action he'd have to swallow it.

Fortunately, there wasn't much of that action left. The man from Philly knew just what to do. He went right to work on the blind side, hitting Dad five, six, seven straight, stiff times in the eye. He wasn't boxing my father anymore, or even whipping him. It was a beating. Beating my father. Beating him.

As the referee stepped close, getting ready to stop it, Dad did what instinct tells the fighter to do—tie the guy up. He reached out, groping, clutching, trying to put a hug on the man from Philadelphia. But he couldn't see him as he took one more, then another shot to the side of the head. He had no mouthpiece now, as one vicious hook ripped it out and sent it ten rows into the seats.

By the time the referee jumped in and wrapped up my father, holding his head warmly as if *he* were the father, Monty had jumped up and started running out. I tried to grab him from my seat, but he punched my hand away and was gone. Archie turned to watch him go, then stared at the door for a minute afterward. He turned back to the TV, pointed the remote, and rewound the tape.

"Well, I done my job good this time, Georgie, didn't I?" Archie said. Something in the sound of his grown man's voice cracking was frightening. "He ain't gonna be back here no more," he whispered, every word quieter than the last.

Almost in an instant, the tape was rewound. The fight had seemed a lot longer than it was. He started it again. "You wanna hear the funniest part?" he said as the two fresh fighters stood in the center of the ring again. "He *won* that fight, your old man. The other guy was busted with half the horsehair removed from his gloves, so they disqualified him. He broke his hands—both of 'em— on your tough old dad's head." He paused, nodded a bunch of times. "Know this, Georgie: It can be a hard thing sometimes to tell winnin' from losin'."

As I stood to go, I could finally feel my body under me again. My face, and the front of my shirt, were soaked. "Ya, that's funny, Arch," I said.

What was funnier to me, but not funny enough to make me smile, was that after all that time Dad finally got to finish our lessons.

I left Archie watching the fight again. "I miss him already," he called without taking his eyes off the screen.

I found him on the floor of the closet. I squatted in front of him.

"You want to talk about it?" I said. He shook his head no.

"Come on," I said. "Let's go out back." He shook his head no. I nodded my head yes.

"Get the hell out of here," he said, and kicked me. I fell backward and he pulled the door closed on himself. I stood, opened the door, and held out my hand to him. He took it, and I pulled him up.

"It's called 'chin music,'" I said as we circled each other in the ring.

"What are you talking about?"

"That's right, you wouldn't know it, it's not a fight term. Chin music, you know, in baseball. Pitcher sends you a message pitch to warn you. Throws the ball near your head. You get the message, step away from the plate, you'll be okay. You don't get the message, you *lose* your head."

"Chin music," he echoed as he threw a left jab that rang off my forehead.

"Nice shot. You want to talk about it now?"

"It was a left jab."

"You know what I mean."

"No, I don't want to talk about it."

He stepped up and threw two into my ribs to make sure I understood. Before he left I threw two back. It sounded like somebody beating a rug. We danced some. I stepped up and whistled one by his ear. He slipped it without hardly moving. Then, *he* was stalking *me*. I backpedaled, threw some jabs, tried to go sideways like I'd done to him a billion times before. He cut the ring off on me, made me fight out of the triangle instead of the square. So I stopped at the turnbuckle and made my stand, planting my feet and firing away—hooks, upper-cuts, hammer shots, the whole show.

I missed. Every single time. He dropped his hands just low enough to look tempting, then did his snake thing, twisting, slithering, bending mad-deningly beyond my reach. I couldn't hit him, couldn't hit Monty no matter how hard I tried.

And I made the key mistake. Lesson ten. No matter what goes wrong, don't let it show. I know he saw it on my face, how stunned I was. So he struck. *Wham-wham*. Two malicious right hooks to my kidney brought my hands down; then a wind-mill, overhand left, came hammering straight down, caught my bottom teeth, drove my chin into my collarbone.

I looked up at my brother from my seat in a puddle. It had rained earlier, and it was coming again. He had become what ESPN would call the Complete Package. He could hit hard, could hit quick, could use both hands. He could slip a punch and he could take one.

Monty didn't gloat over me, even though it was something he'd been waiting a lifetime to do. Instead, he just stared down at me. He let his hands fall to his sides, then shook them until the old hockey gloves, first left, then right, fell to the ground. I saw the fight going on behind his eyes. Finally, against all his training, he cried.

I stood up, shook off my gloves, and went to him. I hugged him around his big head like the referee had done to say, "It's over." I didn't yak at him. When Monty was ready, we just headed back up the stairs. We left the gloves there on the ground, where they could rot in the coming rain.